THE LORD HAVE MERCY

The married life of Robert Mansbridge and his wife Editha is the talk of the village. Whispers of infidelity and wantonness abound; whilst most of their neighbours respect the doctor, Editha is regarded as a shrew. Meanwhile, timid Catherine Duncton is hopelessly in love with Robert, but chained to her invalid father; and sculptor Leslie Crispin carries a torch for Editha. Then Editha dies in mysterious circumstances, and the rumour mill churns ever faster and more fiercely . . .

SHELLEY SMITH

THE LORD HAVE MERCY

Complete and Unabridged

LINFORD
Leicester

First published in Great Britain

First Linford Edition
published 2017

A catalogue record for this book is available
from the British Library.

ISBN 978–1–4448–3312–6

1

A Wet Sunday Afternoon in June

There is nothing more dispiriting than an English village on a wet Sunday afternoon in June. The houses, darkened with rain, stand forlorn against a drab sky. Not so much as a thread of smoke unreels from the chimneys to promise life and comfort within (because it is June, and somewhere, at some time, someone has laid it down that, however cold the weather, fires in summer are an indulgence not to be considered). One might fancy the village abandoned, waiting to be drowned fathoms deep beneath the flooding waters of a dam.

Round the famous green, the lime trees shiver ceaselessly in the fine summer rain …

The shop windows have nothing to reflect but the lowering sky; there is not a dog to be seen in the streets. Or there might just be a stray dog — a fox terrier, say, his coat stiff with moisture, scurrying down the deserted High Street with his head down, too joyless or too busy about his private affairs even to pause for the delightful savour of lamp-posts as he patters by.

A bus lumbers up the sloping road and draws to a halt. A person in a transparent mac scrambles out and without a glance round disappears down a side-turning.

Then silence again, except for the gentle rustle of rain among the leaves.

Over the Bank house garden wall, the chestnut blossoms drop suddenly, silently, like tears, onto the pavement below ...

A car hisses along the wet road. In the house on the corner the old maid draws aside the curtain to look.

'There goes the doctor,' observes Miss Seymour, rubbing her chilly hands one against the other.

★　★　★

Catherine Duncton, on her way to the post with a scarf folded over her hair, saw the doctor's car, saw him raise his hand in salute as he passed; and, in her eagerness to return the greeting, clumsily knocked down a shower of wet hawthorn petals from the branch just above her head. They fell on her like confetti over a bride, fluttering on to her shoulders, clinging in her hair; and like a bride she stood there blushing as she watched the car out of sight. Then, brushing a damp petal from her cheek, she went on her way.

★ ★ ★

'You're in my light again, Mother,' Lucien complained. 'Must you stand by the window? I shouldn't have thought there was anything to see on a day like this.'

'I'm like Keats,' said Mrs. Verney. 'I can peck about the gravel with sparrows. But as it happens I was watching something very interesting: I was observing poor Kate mooning after her love, with all her passion naked on her face.'

'Who?' said Lucien, absorbed in the plans on his drawing board.

'Darling, why don't you listen? I'm talking about Catherine Duncton, the little soul across the way.'

'I realize that, Mother dear. I'm not an

3

imbecile. I understood you to say she was in love with someone. And, merely in order to carry my burden of the conversation civilly and appropriately, so that you should see I was paying attention, I inquired who the man was.'

'The doctor, darling.'

'Oh. Married!' he commented without enthusiasm.

'Of course. She's been devoted to him for years, poor wretch. How pathetic a hopeless love is! Though I suppose it's better than not being in love at all.'

'Why should you suppose that, you dear sentimental old lavender mother? I can't imagine a more ghastly waste of spirit.'

'It's better to feel than not to feel, surely? It's better to know you're alive than to suspect you're half-dead.'

'Why is one more alive when wallowing in emotion?' he asked, idly and not very clearly through the pencil in his jaws. He removed the impediment and glanced up for a moment. 'Does the girl think so too?'

'I've no idea. I've been too discreet to broach the subject to her. The silly child imagines it's a secret.'

'She must be silly indeed if she fancies one can have any privacy, mental or emotional, in a place like this where the people make it their business to find out everything they can about everyone, from the state of one's bank balance to the condition of one's soul. And what they can't find out, they appear to invent.'

'We're interested in people, my pet,' said his mother, lightly brushing his hair up the wrong way as she passed. 'That's something you can never understand.'

'No, I really can't. The febrile curiosity of the rustic mind baffles me. I mean, why bother? People are all exactly alike, I find.'

'Poor little boy,' said his mother. 'You'd better have the light on; you can't see,' she added, fetching the green-shaded lamp. 'If only she had a little more 'go',' Mrs. Verney continued, reverting to Catherine, 'she'd be someone for you to go about with occasionally. She's really quite pretty.'

This was a piece of fatuity best ignored in Lucien's view.

'But what hope is there for her with that

bloody old man?' Eve Verney said, and shook out a cigarette from the packet on the chimney shelf and lit it. The flame danced back at her from the silvery dusk of the convex mirror in its gilt frame: she saw herself, for a match-length of time, sweetly diminished — a fairy woman, and her miniature son with ivory profile and pale hair gilt beneath the lamp. 'She'll never get away from him. That's what's so tragic. Even when he dies at last, he'll go on wrecking her life because she'll never be able to break away emotionally from the father-image. It's Kismet! My God,' said Mrs. Verney with an inspired face, 'I suddenly believe in Kismet. I see what it means.'

'Destiny, so I have always understood.'

'Yes, yes, exactly — Destiny! One creates one's future in the pattern of one's past — unconsciously, of course, but that is why it is irrevocable. Can't you see? It's typical for her to choose someone utterly hopeless to fall in love with; she doesn't want to face adult problems like marriage. She wants to go on being a daughter all her life.'

'Now I'm afraid my little woman is talking balderdash,' her son lilted.

6

'No, I'm not.' Mrs. Verney, excited by her own brilliance, dragged at her cigarette and puffed a cloud of smoke at the ceiling. 'It's the father-image again. She's obsessed by it.'

Surprised into attention, Lucien looked up from his drawing board and said, 'You can't tell me she's in love with that old man!'

'What old man?'

'Dr. Horace.'

'My precious boy, don't be dull! Poor old Horace is at least a hundred. What could have given you that idea? It's Dr. Mansbridge, of course.'

'You said a father-image, Mother o' mine.'

'Well, wouldn't you call him a father-image? He must be all of forty-five.'

Lucien appeared to consider.

'Technically he could just be her father then, I suppose, if he conceived her when he was seventeen. In that case it is hardly likely that she would have been born in wedlock, since the earliest marrying age for males in this country averages twenty-five, I understand.'

'Darling, this horrible donnish sort of humour is growing on you. Be careful!'

'Dear Mama,' said Lucien. He put down his pencil and stretched back in his chair with a yawn. 'I believe you've made up the whole thing. It sounds to me like the lubricous fantasy of a female at the menopause.'

'Lucien! That's rude and not funny,' said Mrs. Verney, flushing.

'Sorry, Mama,' he said airily. Lucien regarded his mother — indeed, all women — as something of a joke.

He was agreeably conscious of her hostile stare.

'You really are becoming quite detestable, my dear boy; you should try and do something about it before it's too late.'

'But isn't it splendid fun for you to have a thoroughly unsatisfactory son to gloom over? If there were time enough and energy to spare, I really would endeavour to do something scandalous for your stupefaction.'

'Isn't that exactly what I'm complaining about, my precious child, your horrible prosing dullness? I can't think why all you young people are so boring nowadays.'

'Silly Mama,' said her son lightly, 'we

8

have supped our fill of horrors. But do go on about Miss Duncton's frustrated sex-life. Has she written to Auntie Mollie of *Weary Women* for advice on her little problem?'

'It grieves me that a son of mine should be too stupid to respect a genuine passion,' Mrs. Verney said in a cold voice.

Lucien smiled. Passion, he did not believe in, taking it to be a fad of idle minds. Carefully, he adjusted his T-square on the drawing.

'Why, I believe I've offended the little woman,' he said cheerfully, 'but how was I to know she took this nonsense seriously?'

Really, Lucien could be very irritating with his maddening assumption of superiority. With the unfailing optimism of mothers, Mrs. Verney hoped, without the least encouragement, that he would grow out of it soon.

★   ★   ★

The doctor's car passed the house in the High Street, with the bow windows full of Staffordshire dogs and copper warming-pans and the iron sign creaking out

'Antiques' in Gothic letters, at the precise moment that Leslie Crispin opened the attic casement to eject a cigar butt. The car sped down the road and Crispin gazed after it thoughtfully.

The light fell bleakly through the glass roof on the huge sculptures below. Larger than life, with seal-like heads and monstrous limbs, it was their vague resemblance to human beings which gave them so terrifying an aspect — like a threat, or a prophecy of some new race. Repellent though they were, there was something suggestively ominous in their quiet strength. They were kin in their potency to an African fetish or an Easter Island image. But if they were considered queer, it was as nothing to the queerness of their creator — a subject for mirth and sniggering behind fingers. With her cigars and her male attire, she was considered a little cracked. But because she was rich and inclined to extravagance, the villagers were careful to be scrupulously respectful to her face; there is nothing crackpot about money, wealth can always acquire its price in respect.

Having burnished her cropped hair,

knotted a silk handkerchief about her throat and thrust on her hand a ring with a stone as big as a cockroach, she slung a jacket on her shoulders, ran quietly down the stairs and threaded through the furniture looming darkly at the back of the shop. China shepherdesses and a set of green wineglasses shook minutely at her tread.

At the door she paused fatally to light a cigarette, and in that moment a cry came from the rear of the house. 'Is that you, darling?'

Crispin made no answer. Tautly, gently, she pressed the door handle down: but it was too late. With a cry of 'Crispin?' her friend, Naomi Ryder, appeared in the doorway, her cheeks flushed, her dark hair wild.

'Oh, darling,' she wailed when she saw her, 'you're not going out?'

Crispin flung a hand up to her brow with a martyred face.

'It's my head. I simply have to get some air.'

'But, darling, tea's nearly ready. Won't you wait? It's such a vile day that I thought I'd knock you up a batch of those tea-cakes you're so fond of.'

'I'll have them when I get back.'

'Oh, they won't be fit to eat then. You know they need to be eaten while they're still hot and fresh.'

Crispin gave a great sigh.

'I'm sorry. I'm sorry.'

'It doesn't matter,' the other said in tones that plainly belied her words. 'Only you might just have thought to let me know you wouldn't be in.'

'My dear, aren't you being a little unreasonable? How was I to know I'd have a headache?'

Naomi shrugged, nursing her grievance.

'Oh, they can easily be thrown away,' she said.

Crispin muttered something between her teeth as she turned impatiently away and opened the door.

'You won't forget we're going to the Ambroses,' Naomi said in a small voice.

'I had not forgotten.'

'I just wondered what time you'd be back.'

'I'm afraid I've no idea.'

Naomi blinked: 'Now you're cross,' she remarked in a tone that sounded more reproachful than penitent, though it was penitence that drove her nervously on.

Crispin said with exquisite precision:

'I simply wanted to go for a walk, because I happen to have a headache. If I had dreamed for an instant it would lead to all this commotion and argument, I would never have attempted anything so audacious.'

'Forgive me, darling,' Naomi said in a husky voice. 'I'm sorry I made such a fuss. It was stupid of me. Of course you must go out if you feel like it, I was being ridiculous.' She hesitated, and then flushing said, 'If you can wait just a moment, I'll get my mac and come with you: Belinda needs a walk.'

Now it was Crispin who flushed.

'But this is persecution! Am I not even to go out alone now? What do you suppose I'm going to do on a Sunday afternoon?'

'Why, I simply thought — ' began the other in genuine bewilderment.

'I want to be *alone.* Can't you understand?'

Naomi's eye at last touched on the venetian-red silk handkerchief, the cornelian ring, and her cheeks reddened. She forced herself to speak calmly but her heart was raging within her.

'Oh, yes, I understand now, don't worry. It was in all innocence though that I offered to come with you; I thought you might be glad of my company. But I see now that it isn't *my* company you're after. What a blind idiot I am, aren't I? Anyone else would have realized at once why you were trying to sneak out of the house without my seeing you.'

'I'm afraid I've not the least idea what you're talking about.'

'Oh, don't lie! It's so stupid. You know I always find you out. As if I didn't know you are going to see that woman.' Foolish tears sprang to her eyes. 'If only you wouldn't *lie* to me about it. That's what I can't bear!'

'You force me to lie, my dear, because otherwise your insane jealousy makes it impossible for me to get out of the house without a degrading scene.'

'Why should you imagine I care where you go or whom you see? It's nothing to me. It simply makes me laugh. If you want so much to be with that woman all the time, why on earth don't you go to her? Why not go and live with *her* — if she'll have you — and then you won't have to endure these degrading scenes and you won't be forced to lie your way out of them,' Naomi stuttered.

'You don't know how you tempt me,' said Crispin, smiling coldly.

'Well, why don't you go, then? What's keeping you? You needn't think I want you to stay; I wish to God you would go. I wish to God I'd never met you!'

'A little late to think of that now.'

'Yes. You've ruined my life! My God, when I think of how I've slaved for you! Cooking, cleaning, waiting on you hand and foot, so that nothing should interfere with your precious work.'

'No one asked you to. Why did you do it if it was so distasteful?'

'Because I believed in you,' Naomi said in a trembling voice. 'I didn't want thanks, but everyone likes to be appreciated a little. You take it all for granted. You never think of anyone but yourself. You never think how hard it's sometimes been to keep this place going and run my business too. Of course, *my* work doesn't count; it's not *art*. If I miss an important sale, that's just too bad.

15

It's never entered your head to try to make things a bit easier for *me.* If you're left to wash a teacup you grumble for hours.'

'Must we go through this old hoop again?' said Crispin with her eyes closed. 'If I was not paying you enough, you had only to say.'

Naomi laughed.

'Money can't pay for what I've given you. That sort of service can't be bought. See if she'll do as much for you. Ask *her* to run about after you and pick your clothes off the floor,' Naomi said and gave a sharp mirthless laugh like a jay's cry.

'Oh, how your vulgarity grates on my nerves,' Crispin complained with a sort of rage. 'You hoard up every little thing you've ever done for me, like a miser, until you can bring it out years later to use against me. It's so common, so mean. I can't stand such pettiness! I can't stand these rows, I warn you!'

'Well, go, then!' Naomi cried hoarsely with a trembling lip and a wild gleam in her eye. 'Why don't you go?'

'I'm going,' said Crispin lightly. And went.

Naomi leaned against the closed door and put her wet face on her arm.

'Damn Editha! Damn her! Oh, damn her! I wish she was dead!'

For it was Editha she blamed, not Crispin; Editha with her cruel indifference (her very indifference to someone with Crispin's genius and charm was an affront).

Editha was Mrs. Mansbridge, the doctor's wife.

She had taken Crispin's eye at last year's Autumn Flower Show, looking very cool and bored among the hot, flushed people pressing eagerly round the exhibits. She was a pale, aloof woman, whose large, feverishly dark eyes seemed to burn with an intense contempt for whatever they saw.

Mrs. Doctor was not popular. Apart from a few toadies in the local Conservative Women's Association, of which she was president, people did not cotton to her. She was tolerated because of her husband. He was liked; an agreeable, good-humoured chap. What did not go well was her habit of bullying her husband in public. It embarrassed people and made them sorry for him, and that did his practice no good. The last thing anyone wants is a doctor one pities; a doctor must be a kind of god, since at some time he may hold one's life in his hands.

Sixteen years ago, when Dr. Mansbridge first came to the village and bought the uninhabitable old stone house in the High Street and put up his brass plate, he had had to fight a great deal of prejudice and resentment against him as an intruder. It was considered bad taste to plant himself on the village without respect to the doctor already practising there. They tried to freeze him out. They did not want that type of person in their renowned and ancient village. But, starting with a few casualties among the working class, he gradually became accepted; and, since he was a good doctor, his popularity increased.

Dr. and Mrs. Mansbridge had been married eighteen years. If it was a disappointment to him that there were no children, he was too much of an extrovert to do other than take life as it came.

It was not her childlessness that had soured Mrs. Mansbridge, it was life itself: life had not come up to her expectations; life had let her down. Inwardly she was consumed with a perpetual rage against the waste, the injustice, of finding herself in middle life buried in this deadly little village with no hope of escape. Inside her hands faint scars were to be seen where boredom had so frequently made her grind her nails into their palms, at village routs or cocktail parties among the gentry, at meals alone with her husband and in bed at night when he made love to her.

★ ★ ★

Catherine Duncton, returning from the post, saw 'that awful sculptress person' mounting the steps of the old stone house. That meant she must be going to visit Mrs. Mansbridge; she always went when the doctor was not there. Catherine noted the fact with pious satisfaction. The more items she could tot up against Mrs. Mansbridge as a wilfully neglectful wife, the less hopeless did she herself feel, and the more excusable was her own guilt. It was wrong to love a married man, she knew that, but she could no more stifle her thoughts about him than she could voluntarily cease to breathe: she could only long for his wife somehow to be taken out of their way, for she simply could not believe that he could love a woman so universally disliked. She went no further than that even in her thoughts, for she was a good girl: one of those good girls who quietly and honourably lead unbearable lives. There is always at least one to be found in every village, tied by duty or devotion to some elderly relative. Catherine had an invalid father; she used to tell herself with obstinate loyalty that it was only natural for him to be irascible and unjust, cooped up as he was day after day by his lattice window.

And then, in the irrational way of human passion, one fine day she found herself violently in love with this Dr. Mansbridge, whom she had seen around since she was a little girl.

She and her father had always gone to Dr. Horace, and there could be no question of changing doctors — her father disapproved of this 'new' man, as he chose still to regard him. So for nearly two years all her love had to feed on were chance glimpses of Dr. Mansbridge caught in street or shop, with never a word exchanged because they had never met socially; though sometimes, catching her stare, he would raise his hat vaguely.

Until three months ago.

★   ★   ★

Editha was painting her nails for the Ambroses' cocktail party that evening. She did not look up when Crispin came in. Only she jerked away sharply and said, 'Don't!' as Crispin dropped a light caress on her head in passing. 'I can't bear anyone touching my hair!'

'I once had an aunt whose proud boast it was that her husband had never seen her with her hair down. It gave one a very odd idea of their private life, I always thought,' Crispin said, dropping on her knees before the little fire cheerfully rubbing its flames together.

Editha unwillingly allowed herself to laugh.

Pleased, Crispin put out a hand; and at once Editha uttered a sharp cry of vexation: 'Mind, you'll smudge my nails!'

'Sorry, darling. Beautiful nails! Let me

have a look at them. Why not? I'm not going to steal them … Oh, very well. Tell me what you've been doing all this vile day.'

'Nothing.'

'Then you should be a teeny bit pleased to see me.'

Editha waved a hand vaguely in the air to dry the lacquer and made no reply.

Crispin said doubtfully, 'I hope you didn't mind me turning up uninvited, but I saw Robert's car dashing off somewhere, and I thought you might be feeling a bit lonely.' She gave the other woman a mischievous glance.

Editha patted away a yawn.

'Not in the least,' she said ambiguously.

'Tired, dearest?'

'Not in the least,' she repeated.

'Then what's the matter?'

'Only bored.'

'Oh, you poor dear, of course you are. It's cruel to shut a woman like you away from life. I don't know how you stick it. How I long to take you away from it all,' she said fiercely, hugging her knees.

Editha smiled faintly.

'Has it escaped your notice that I have a

husband, by chance?'

'Is it important?'

'To me, very. I happen to be rather fond of him.'

'You said just now you were bored.'

'My dear woman, wasn't it rather presumptuous of you to suppose I was referring to Robert? I assure you I was speaking merely for the moment.'

'You mean, I bore you?'

Editha made no reply. She appeared to be absorbed in screwing the brush back into the bottle of nail lacquer.

'I'm sorry.' Crispin stood up. 'Perhaps you'd like me to go?'

Editha leaned back, smiling, and languidly said:

'How absurdly touchy you are! You never seem to know when you are being teased.'

'Your teasing rather stings.'

'It's meant to.'

'Why? Do you like wounding people?'

'If you can't amuse me, I must amuse myself. Before you sit down again, you might touch the bell. I presume you want to stay to tea; and tea may stimulate you to be a little more entertaining.'

Editha was dressed for the cocktail party, her narrow form pacing restlessly about the bedroom, when at last the doctor returned.

'You're terribly late,' she greeted him peevishly.

'Couldn't help it, my dear. I'm lucky to be back as soon as this, as a matter of fact; there was an obstruction in the uterus, and it meant — '

'Oh, spare me the obstetrical horrors, *please*!' she cried, tapping her foot, as she stood by the dressing-table, trying on rings and discarding them.

He undid his tie, whistling a cheerful stave.

'For God's sake, hurry,' she said, eyeing him irritably. 'We shall be the last to arrive. Not that I care. So far as I'm concerned, the later we're there the sooner we can get away. But you know what the Ambroses are; there won't be anything left to drink if we don't get there soon. They never allow for more than two drinks apiece.'

Her husband said mildly, 'It's really

better for you not to drink.'

She gave a short laugh.

'What is a little pain, compared with the agony of boredom it would be without a drink or two to liven it up?'

'If you feel like that about them, it would surely have been simpler to refuse their invitation,' he said, feeling his jaw to see whether he needed to shave. He did. But he decided he would rather go looking less-than-immaculate than increase Editha's irritation by keeping her waiting while he shaved.

'Odd as it may seem to you, Robert dear,' Editha said with her bitter smile, 'I do try to build you up socially — always in the pitiful fond hope that it won't be just so much wasted effort.'

'You should have given up years ago trying to make a silk purse of me, my dear; you'll never succeed. Is this the only clean shirt I've got?'

She sprayed scent against her throat.

'If it's the only one there, that would seem the obvious deduction.' Her foot recommenced its impatient tapping. 'And do for God's sake hurry, Robert!'

* * *

By the time the Mansbridges arrived, people were already beginning to leave. Mrs. Ambrose came forward with a distracted smile, thinking with dismay, as she greeted them, that this would mean another half-hour at least.

Dr. Mansbridge said, 'I'm sorry we're so terribly late.'

'We thought you weren't coming.' Mrs. Ambrose looked round for her husband. 'James, do get Mrs. Mansbridge and the doctor a drink.'

'Robert's fault as usual,' Editha said pleasantly. She glanced about the room and saw that there was no one of any interest. She knew them all and there was not one among them whom she cared to talk to.

Robert went across to where Mr. Lawrence, a retired stockbroker, was deep in conversation with old General Ridley on the enthralling subject of lawn fertilizers: lawns are a passion with retired gentlemen who live in the country.

Mr. Ambrose brought Mrs. Doctor a tepid martini and stood beside her making polite remarks, to which the lady replied in unenthusiastic monosyllables, drooping her lids and ceaselessly tapping at the ash of her cigarette. He was thankful when, after a few endless minutes, Leslie Crispin came over and released him.

'I'd almost given you up, darling. What kept you?'

'Oh, Robert makes a habit of being late on these occasions.' She laughed. 'I suppose he hopes people will notice it and think what a clever busy little man he is. I don't know why I bother to come.' She finished her drink with a disgusted face.

There were several men in the room, and uninteresting though they undoubtedly were, it irked her immensely that not one of them chose to come and talk to her. She stared into her empty glass sulkily. 'What does one have to do to get a drink in this house? Swear an affidavit or something?'

I'll get you one. Wait there. I won't be a minute.'

For approximately a minute, Editha did remain where she was, because she could not decide which group to join. Then she went over to where Mr. Golding, the schoolmaster, leaned against the bookcase talking to his wife.

'My good people,' she said brightly, 'the bedroom is the place for marital confidences. You have not come here to talk to one another. You are neglecting your duties.'

Mrs. Doctor's humour never seemed very amusing: it must have been the way it was delivered. Mr. Golding turned on her a look of keen distaste: he knew her of old.

'But your glass is empty,' he cried, seizing it. 'You must let me get you a drink,' and, caddishly abandoning his poor wife, he bolted.

There was a small uneasy silence. And then young Mrs. Golding said nervously:

'Hasn't it been a dreadful day?'

'Really? In what way?'

'Well, I mean — the weather ... All this rain.'

Mrs. Mansbridge said pleasantly:

'Do you know, by the time I've discussed it every day with each individual tradesman, I simply cannot bring myself even to mention the subject again. It's so terribly boring, isn't it?'

Young Mrs. Golding gave a nervous little laugh, feeling, as she was meant to feel, plebeian and dull. She was a pretty girl, with a mass of charmingly wayward hair and a tenderly candid expression. Now, with this horrible woman eyeing her, she felt ill-dressed and untidy and was sure her face needed powdering.

And so far as Mrs. Mansbridge was concerned, she was right: to the doctor's wife, she looked a mess. The touching prettiness of Mrs. Golding's youth left her unmoved; she only thought how stupid she looked in that fussy little frock with her great cow's eyes.

Mrs. Mansbridge began talking about the exhibition of paintings Janet Scott, the art mistress at the school, had recently shown in the village hall.

'She's clever.'

'Yes. And awfully nice,' agreed Mrs. Golding.

'It must make it much more amusing for you to have someone about your own age at the school. She's not exactly pretty, but she has the sort of looks that men find attractive, don't you think?' she said, smiling at Mrs. Golding. 'Of course, she's been here for years and I dare say that partly accounts for her popularity — we're so conservative we can't make up our minds whether we like a person till we've known them at least ten years.' Mrs. Mansbridge laughed. 'We all thought Edward was going to marry her. It was such a surprise for us when he brought you back.'

At this point Crispin came up with a drink for Editha and, since the two women had not met, Editha was obliged to introduce them.

'You've seen her sculpture, of *course*,' she said; which was embarrassing for Mrs. Golding, who hadn't and lacked the *savoir vivre* to know whether she should admit ignorance or pretend she had. Flushing, she murmured something inaudible.

Mrs. Mansbridge then let the conversation drop completely. Her eyes wandered about the room. After a while she said to Crispin, 'I think your little friend wants you. Don't you think you should go back to her? She's been glaring across at me for the last five minutes as if she'd like to kill me.'

('I expect she would, too,' thought young

Mrs. Golding.)

It was then that Naomi came over and, ignoring the other two women, said in the cold commanding tones of a wife with a bone to pick:

'I'm going home.'

Crispin said, 'All right,' making no move.

'Aren't you coming?'

'When I'm ready.'

Editha said:

'You might just as well go now; I'm leaving almost at once.' Thus graciously giving Crispin back to her friend.

Without a word, Naomi turned on her heel and walked away. Her face was crimson and when the vicar's wife spoke to her she walked on without answering, as though she had not heard — or could not trust herself to speak.

Crispin muttered sulkily to her glass, 'I wish you wouldn't interfere, Editha, it only makes matters worse.'

Mrs. Mansbridge arched her brows in cold astonishment.

'Don't blame me, if you please. Why not have gone with her? Go after her now; you can still catch her up if you hurry.'

Mr. Golding returned with the drinks. There was an uncomfortable pause. Most of the guests had left by this time, and there were but a few scattered people beside this awkward little group.

Dr. Mansbridge came over to collect his wife. Seeing her with a fresh drink in her hand, he mildly suggested she should not drink any more. It is doubtful whether anyone heard him, but no one could have helped hearing her answer. She pitched her voice clear and high:

'My dear Robert, please don't behave as if I were an inebriate. Try not to make a fool of yourself before all these good people.'

Robert said in his pleasant, unperturbed way:

'My dear, I only wished to remind you that it would be wiser not to drink any more.'

'Well, kindly allow me to be the best judge of that, and don't be so damned officious.'

He laid a hand gently on hers, and before she could realize his intention he had taken the glass from her and drunk down the contents himself. He met with a twinkle the fury that burned in her look and dyed her throat.

With a laugh of rage Editha turned to the person beside her, who happened to be the vicar's wife, and exclaimed, 'Robert being masterful is a sight to make a cat weep. The worst of having a doctor for a husband is one mayn't even be ill without interference.' (This was the first anyone had heard that Mrs. Doctor was not well.) With her own inimitable brand of rudeness Editha added, 'I don't suppose even your husband fancies himself God more than Robert.'

The vicar's wife murmured something vague at this insult to her husband, and with a kind of jerk the party suddenly broke up.

'Why *do* we ask that woman?' muttered Mrs. Ambrose, as she waved to her departing guests from the doorway.

'Poor chap, it's a bit hard on him if he's to be left out of everything because his wife's intolerable,' said her husband.

'It's his own fault, he never should have married her. I wonder why he ever did?'

'She must have been a very handsome girl. I suppose he was in love with her. He may still be.'

'Poor devil!' said Mrs. Ambrose, closing the front door.

2

An Apron Stained with Blood

Mrs. Verney woke with a penetrating sense of having just escaped from something disagreeable, and lay for a moment staring out at the stars as faint as specks of eggshell in the mild midsummer sky. Some intangible wisp of emotion from her dream still floated at the edge of her consciousness … Something horrid … Catherine Duncton in a bloodstained blue apron appeared in her mind, smiling a strange accusing smile at Mrs. Verney as she leaned forward with the knife in her heart.

Mrs. Verney snapped on the bedside lamp and fumbled for a cigarette. She watched the smoke drift beyond the pool of light to the great beams jutting from the shadows. Of course she had dreamed of Catherine because she had been talking about her with Lucien, and because of his abominable tiresomeness she had not finished her story, and so it came twisting into her dreams. That was all it was.

But it had been something more than just a ludicrous nightmare ... the bloodstained blue apron ... the knife ... those she knew, those had been real. And they brought back to her recollection, with a quite horrible new emphasis, that day last spring, in the kitchen at Honeysuckle Cottage, talking to Catherine as she peeled apples in her blue apron.

Mrs. Verney had been talking in her lively intrepid 'modern' way of the need to live more fully, to learn how to get what one wanted from life and not just let it dribble dully away. It was a sin against life, she believed, not to use every moment of it, not to squeeze it like an orange and wring out every last drop. And so on. She had been thinking less of Catherine's problems, of which she was hardly aware, than of her problem son: so good and hard-working, 'never a day's anxiety' to her — except that at twenty-eight he was already as dry as a picked bone. And Catherine had listened as if she were being lectured, thinking, no doubt, that it was all very well for people

36

to *talk.*

'I wish you'd take Lucien in hand, Catherine, and wake him up a bit,' Mrs. Verney had said; for Catherine, though heavy in the hand, was so safe and malleable, just the sort of girl she could use to start breaking down Lucien's absurd resistance to women.

'Me?' said Catherine, amazed. 'I'm hopeless with young men. Lucien doesn't even know I'm alive.'

Eve Verney had laughed.

'My dear child, it's your job to make him realize that you're alive. No man can resist a woman if she puts her mind to it; if she really wants him he doesn't stand a chance.'

Catherine had said earnestly, as though she really needed to know: 'But how? How can one do that?'

'Get in his way, trip over his feet, force yourself on him till he becomes aware of you,' Mrs. Verney had advised with a smile, never dreaming that the situation was other than totally imaginary.

Catherine murmured, 'I thought men hated to be run after.'

'You mustn't run after them, my dear;

that would never do. But if women didn't know how to make men conscious of them there'd never be any marriages, believe me,' Mrs. Verney had assured her.

Catherine didn't answer. She was staring out at the leaf-chequered lane, rustling and blinking in the dancing spring light, to where a car stood at the corner outside the Misses Seymour's house. Mrs. Verney followed her gaze.

Suddenly Catherine had uttered a stifled cry. Mrs. Verney turned and saw with horror Catherine holding up her hand with the sharp little kitchen knife stuck an inch deep in the fleshy part of her hand beneath the thumb.

'Look what I've done!' she said in a foolish voice.

The sight of blood always sickened Mrs. Verney, and before she could bring herself to move, the girl herself had pulled out the blade and wrapped her blue apron round her hand. The blood spread in dark blots against the blue in a manner that Mrs. Verney found terrifying.

'It's all right,' Catherine had insisted with the strangest smile, her eyes glittering. 'It'll be all right.'

'But you must have it seen to,' she had protested. 'It'll have to be stitched. Shall I go with you to the doctor?'

'The doctor's just down the lane at Ivybank, I noticed his car. Perhaps you wouldn't mind ... ' the girl had said breathlessly.

And that was how Dr. Mansbridge and the girl first met.

And only now the question projected itself disagreeably in Mrs. Verney's mind that because of her foolish talk the girl had deliberately injured herself to engineer the meeting. But the notion was too fantastic, Mrs. Verney protested; people didn't do such things. It couldn't be true; such things only happened in Russian novels. It was her bad dream that had put the idea in her head.

★ ★ ★

The morning promised an exquisite day. Since dawn the rooks had been racketing in the ilex tree behind the Seymours' house, flopping heavily in tattered black bundles through the branches and soaring back again with angry caws. In the stillness and sharp morning light with its heavy shadows, the clustered village looked as quaint and unreal as a film set.

Workmen on bicycles began to bowl down the empty streets on their way to work. The bird-twittering tranquillity was pierced suddenly by the scream and whine of a circular saw in the wood yard. The day had begun.

In the lonely cottage on the hill, the spinster performed her ritual observances on her knees. The cottage was so old that the windows were down by the floor and one could not see out unless one got down on one's knees. She turned the black object in her hands slowly this way and that. This moment for her was the crown of the day. She committed it always with the sense of guilt we all feel for our secret vices, and yet she could not forego its peculiar pleasure. It was an error of taste, yes, she admitted it, but what harm did it do? No one knew, thank God … !

Immense close-ups of sycamore leaves, of telegraph wires, of a woodpecker, came before her eyes; and then, turning carefully, she focussed on the Fitzalans' garden ... What on earth was the Colonel's wife doing, running down the garden in her dressing-gown, bending under branches, smiling to herself, the skirt of her gown dark with dew ... ?

It was delightful to get inside people's houses and watch them when they thought themselves to be unobserved ... There was old General Ridley kneeling by his bed with his face in his hands ... Oh, goodness, and there was that dreadful person, Miss Crispin, walking about her room most disgustingly as naked as the day she was born ...

There was a child with a face like a pillar-box, obviously screaming with all the force of its lungs. Poor little thing, so hideous ... !

Gracious, it must be getting late, for there was Mrs. Ambrose, as punctual as the sun, trotting to the farm to buy her husband's breakfast egg because he liked it new-laid ... It was time for her to get dressed; and with a sigh, Miss Barnaby put away the binoculars her brother, the Commander, had left her. She often wondered whether poor

Andrew knew how much interest they had brought into her life.

$$\star \quad \star \quad \star$$

Lucien Verney, on his way to the station, hurried past the madwoman idling at the roadside with a dog cradled in her arms, averting his eyes from the slimy mouth with the little crest of foam at the corner. She was talking to someone up in the sky, pausing every now and then with her head on one side to listen for their answer, sometimes nodding agreement, sometimes arguing back. She broke off her conversation with the heavenly being to greet Lucien politely.

'Mornin' Mis' Verney!'

He hastened his steps without answering. In a sudden rage she bawled after him: 'Stuck-up bastard!'

Her vituperative yells followed him down the road. He dared not glance behind to see whether the foul fiend was padding after him in her ragged carpet slippers. He thought for the fiftieth time that she ought to be put away: it was outrageous to leave such a creature loose, perhaps to frighten children; she might even become violent and attack someone. He could not understand why no one on the council saw to it. There was no pity in him for her loneliness that had festered into suspicion. Ragged, half-starved, laughed at and tormented by the village children, shunned with horror by the villagers, a derelict hut her home, a scrawny whelp her sole companion, she possessed nothing but her freedom; and Lucien would lightly have taken even that from her.

★   ★   ★

Young Mrs. Golding, as she poured her husband's coffee, said with a smile, 'I had no idea that you were expected to marry Janet.' It struck her as a joke. Something to tease Edward with.

'Hadn't you?' murmured Mr. Golding, sorting his letters.

'Did she expect it too?' she asked, putting the cosy back on the pot.

He said absently, 'I believe she did.'

At these words, to young Mrs. Golding's dismay, a pang of jealousy seemed to pierce her breast. She waited for this odd sensation to die away. She pushed the bacon from her. Why on earth should she be jealous of Janet? It was really too absurd. Yet she could not prevent herself asking — she *had to* know:

'Were you in love with her, then?'

'No. Look, will you tell the matron that Boddy minor has been having trouble with his ears, and his parents want — oh, you'd better show her the letter,' he said, throwing it across to her.

Obediently, she folded it into her pocket. 'Then why should she expect it?'

'What? Who? What are you talking about?'

'Janet,' she said, eyeing him boldly. 'If you were never in love with her, how could she have imagined you were likely to marry her?'

He was lighting his pipe, sucking at the flame noisily. He said, in jerky intervals, 'She — fancied herself — in love with me — I believe.'

Mrs. Golding looked down at her hands in her lap.

'Then it must have been a nasty shock for her when you came back with me this term.'

'No. Why? She knew perfectly well that I should never marry her; my intentions had been quite clear.'

Young Mrs. Golding sat quite still and said nothing. 'I'm not so stupid that I can't understand the implications behind your remark,' she said to him in her head. But her ideas were whirling and dashing about so fast that she hardly knew what she thought. When she was quite sure she had control over her voice, she said:

'It had got as far as that?'

'What?' said Mr. Golding, absorbed once more in his letters.

'It had got, I mean, to the point where you actually had to tell her you didn't want to marry her.'

He said easily, 'It was just one of those things. A stupid affair really, born of propinquity. But I suppose we were both bored, there's not much to do here.' He laughed. 'Mind you, she's an amusing girl, Janet; a good sport, and quite attractive in a messy bohemian way; I'm not saying we didn't have a good time together. But it wasn't serious. If she let herself be involved more deeply, that was hardly my fault. I'm not a person to submit to emotional blackmail; that can only end in disaster. Besides, I fancy it's an experience each of us has to go through at some time in our lives; it's part of growing up.' He was thrusting letters back untidily into their envelopes as he spoke. 'I say,' he added suddenly, looking up at his wife, 'don't let Janet know I've discussed it with you, will you? She mightn't like it. Girls are funny.'

'Yes, aren't they?' agreed his wife in a high unnatural voice.

He looked at her, faintly surprised.

His bride was staring at him as if the prince had suddenly turned back into a frog before her eyes.

He thought how lusciously silly she looked with her great eyes as wide as a doll's. He reached over to stroke her delicious forearm, but she drew away.

'No. Wait a moment, Ned.'

'What's the matter, honey?' he said, coming over and slipping a hand beneath the thick fair hair to clasp the back of her neck.

She pulled away from his beguiling touch, wrenching herself round to look at him.

'Ned.' It was difficult to say. 'Was she … ? Were you … ?' she stammered.

He laughed and dropped a kiss on to her hair.

'My darling girl, don't look so horrified! I hope you didn't think I was a virgin when I married you.'

'It's not that, Edward; you don't understand. I mean, of course I knew you must have had other girls. One doesn't think about that; it's the past. But with Janet … Can't you see? It makes it … Oh!' She rose up and stood with her back to him, blindly rearranging the little ornaments on the chimney-shelf, so that he should not see her tears.

'But the whole thing was dead and done with months ago,' he protested. 'I've never given it another thought.'

'But other people have. I don't know how I can bear it,' she muttered with her face in her hands.

'Dear heart, what would you have me do?' he said lightly.

She could not see why he did not understand. Men were different. She tried again.

'You should have made her leave before

47

ever you brought me here.'

'But, darling, how could I make her leave if she wanted to stay? I can't sack her. And I could hardly have gone to the Head and explained the situation to him. I don't think he'd have liked it.'

'It isn't funny,' she said coldly.

'Oh, Bets, *really!*'

'No,' she said, pulling away, 'please don't! Haven't you any imagination? If you can't see how humiliating it is for your wife, can't you see how horrible it must be for Janet?'

He said, quite genuinely:

'Why?'

'Why? Because it seems that everyone in this damned place knows about your hateful *amours,*' she cried, blundering into a chair as she left the room.

⋆   ⋆   ⋆

In the shadowy depths of the mirror Editha's eyes met her reflection as she adjusted her shady hat. She picked up her shopping basket. It was Norah's day out. Editha, too, would have liked to go out instead of having to plan and prepare another

48

dreary meal. It was a day to drive for miles and miles into the country, away from everything — by which she meant herself. She longed passionately to get away from this place full of people rotting away their lives in quiet contentment. But it was her own rotting wasted life that she resented; *they* were more than half-dead already.

She could almost have prayed for something to break the endless monotony, she thought as she crossed the garden, only there was nothing to pray to. She opened the gate and recoiled from the man standing on the step.

'My God!' she exclaimed, with her hand to her throat.

The man grinned.

'No; it's me,' he said, with a twinkle in his round, bloodshot, blue eyes.

He was about forty years of age, with a florid complexion and fairish hair, short and parched-looking. In his atrocious garments and dirty plimsolls he looked for all the world like a shipwrecked sailor (the gallant, honest, derelict who comes to your back door!), with his entire possessions in the brown paper parcel he was carrying tucked under one arm. She said in a low, furious voice: 'What are you doing here?'

'I've come to see you, dear,' he said. 'Don't say you're not pleased to see me, after all this time.'

She said harshly, 'What do you want? If it's money, you've come to the wrong shop. I'm not giving you a penny.'

He gave her a sly look, almost of admiration; but there was mirth in his eye, as if he was laughing at her too. A look that always enraged her to suffocation. 'You always were a hard girl, Ede.'

'Not hard enough where you were concerned. But I am now. I've learned. So be warned.'

But all the time they were exchanging these remarks, her eyes were darting up and down the road outside for fear someone she knew should see her talking to this seedy apparition and begin to wonder. Along came old Miss Duckworth, stumping towards them with her tussore gamp; there was nothing for it but to get him inside, out of her sight. She thanked heaven that Norah was out; not that she had the least intention of letting him into the house, not

50

if she could help it.

He looked about him, very much at his ease.

'Pretty garden,' he said. 'Do you look after it yourself? I could give you a hand with it. I should rather like that. It would help me — to — to — ' He tapped his chest mournfully. 'I don't mind telling you, Ede, I'm in pretty poor shape. The old boy can't last long.'

She looked at him with scorn.

'Don't take me for a fool,' she said.

He dropped on to the grass and unbuttoned his threadbare overcoat with a contented expression. He had dropped the 'dying man' gambit instantly, seeing it was no use; he never wasted time trying to save his face.

'Ah, this is the life for me,' he exclaimed, turning his face up to the sun. 'Come and sit down,' he added, patting the ground beside him. 'Why not be matey?'

'Because I don't feel matey, Harry. I've no time to waste. Tell me what you've come for.'

He lay back and put his hands beneath his head.

'All right,' he said easily. 'I'll tell you. I'd like to rest here quietly for a bit. I want a chance to look around me and get on my feet; I've never had a decent break in my life. I wouldn't be any trouble; I shouldn't expect to be introduced to your friends. You could pretend I was the gardener or the boot boy.'

He looked up at her in sudden alarm as she dropped beside him, dragging at his lapels as she hissed:

'Now what is it? What have you done this time? Are the police looking for you? I want the truth.'

He flummoxed her by bursting into laughter.

'What a fool you are, Ede,' he said merrily. 'If I wanted to hide from the police, do you think I'd come to you? Coo, lumme!' he exclaimed in his vulgar way. 'That would be a showdown!' He chuckled. 'I only offered to keep out of the way of your friends because I know what a blasted snob you are, old Ede. I know I'm not respectable. I know I'm not fit to be seen like this; but to tell you the truth, I haven't a rag to my back bar what I stand up in. Not so much as a bloody pair of socks, boo-hoo!' He stuck his leg up in the air so that the frayed trouser cuff slid away to expose a bare, dirty ankle. 'I expect Robert has some old socks and a shirt or two he wouldn't miss. I don't mind them being worn, I'm not fussy.'

Editha stood up.

'I'll look through his things and see what he can spare. But you can't stay here. That's definite.'

'Well, that's up to you, old girl,' he said, and shrugged as though it didn't matter a rap.

'Robert would never permit it,' she said.

He gave her a dry, knowing glance.

'Poor old Robert!'

His condescension infuriated her. It was maddening that he never believed a word she said. She detested him, lolling there so shamelessly at her feet.

'What do you suggest I should do, then?' he said, limply putting his soul into her hands as he always did.

'I don't give a damn what you do! You've made your own life. It doesn't concern me.'

'The fact is, my darling sister,' he said, the blade of grass between his lips wagging as he spoke, 'that I ain't got nowhere else to go, and I'm stony broke.' Languidly, he rolled his hips from side to side, pulling out his pocket linings to show there was nothing in them but fluff.

'You can't stay here,' she repeated.

'No?'

'No. You ought to know how people talk in a place like this, and I'm not going to have Robert's reputation spoiled by a lot of mean gossip.'

'Oh, it's Robert you're thinking of, is it?' he said, grinning up at her. 'Still,' he went on, closing his eyes against the sun, 'it wouldn't help Robert's reputation much if his brother-in-law died of starvation and neglect on his doorstep. Would it?' he asked reasonably.

The danger was that Robert might return at any moment. She could not afford to let them meet. Robert was such a weak fool. She took a purse out of her basket and opened it. Her face was stony.

'You can have this. It's all I've got,' she said, and handed him a ten-shilling note.

Very slowly, with a quite expressionless face, he sat up and took the note, slowly examined it, and then very thoughtfully folded it and stowed it away without a word.

'Coo!' he uttered at last in a winded voice. 'I reckon it takes a good deal to surprise me, but when it comes to kicking out your only brother with a ten-shilling note like a beggar, then by God, for sheer heartlessness you've got anything beat that I've ever come across in my rough life.'

It was Editha's turn to laugh.

'Did you really think that because you are my brother I would fall on your neck with joy?' she said contemptuously.

'We were fond of one another as children,' he murmured.

'I don't know what makes people with no morals so sentimental. It's very odd. You mean absolutely nothing to me, except that I'm ashamed of being related to you. So why should you expect me to do anything for you? I gave you that money, which seems to have upset you so, to get rid of you, just as I would to any other beggar.'

'Poor old Robert,' he said, getting to his feet and brushing the bits of grass from his clothes, 'what's he done to deserve a bitch like you? I bet you give him hell. I bet he often wishes he'd settled for a quick martyrdom — say, being crucified and eaten alive by soldier ants.'

Her whole body trembled with rage. 'Get out!' she said.

'What about those things of Robert's before I go?'

'Get out,' she repeated, 'before I lose my temper with you.'

'All right, Ede,' he said quietly, but there was a look in his wild and bloodshot eyes, a tone in his voice, that she did not care for. 'I'm going,' he said, humping his brown paper parcel more securely under his arm, and went.

★   ★   ★

It was too late to go out after that; and besides, she badly needed a drink. It was tiresome that Robert should come in and find her with a glass of whisky in her hand. He always made a quite absurd fuss now if she took a drink.

He glanced at her sharply.

'What's the matter?' he said.

56

She didn't answer.

He put an arm round her shoulder and said more kindly, 'Come on now, old lady, what is it? Feeling rotten? In pain again?'

'I'm always in pain,' she said bitterly, as though it was his fault in some way.

'Then is it a good idea to drink, when you must know by now that it simply aggravates it?' he asked mildly.

'If a whisky and soda can stop me wanting to cut my throat, I think it is.'

'That's a very silly way to talk.'

'You think I don't mean it. You don't know how savagely fed up I get sometimes. What's the use of it all, I think.'

'You must try to bear in mind that this depression is merely a symptom, my dear. Have you been eating anything fatty again?'

'You saw what I had for breakfast,' she said indifferently.

'Nothing since?'

'No.'

'No cream cakes when you were out?' he persisted, knowing what women were.

'I tell you, I've had nothing. It doesn't make a particle of difference, anyway; I'm always in pain,' she said testily.

He observed her professionally as she took the cold joint out of the safe and began carelessly hacking pieces off it. Suddenly she broke the silence to say, without looking at him:

'Would you rather be crucified and eaten alive by ants than married to me, Robert?'

He looked at her in amazement.

'My dear girl, what on earth are you talking about?'

'Our marriage. It hasn't been very successful, I suppose, really.'

'We rub along all right.'

'But underneath you're pretty wretched, are you? Did I ever make you happy? I wonder. You needn't answer that, I'd sooner not know.'

'What an extraordinary conversation,' Robert said in a wondering tone. 'It sounds as if you've been reading some novel.'

'Poor Robert. Never mind. I shall soon be dead. Won't I?' she added, flicking him a glance from the corner of her eye as she prodded the potatoes.

'Oh,' he said on a note of comprehension, 'so that is what all this rigmarole has been leading to. We're back at trying to catch that old bee, are we?'

She smiled wryly.

'You think I don't know what's the matter with me.'

'I know what you *think* is the matter with you. I can never understand why people always jump to the conclusion when they've got a pain that it must be cancer.'

'Can you truthfully swear that it isn't?'

'Good Lord, yes,' he said impatiently.

But she didn't really believe him. She knew that doctors always lied. She said, in so low a voice that he could hardly catch the words:

'I don't want to die like that, Robert. I'd kill myself sooner.'

'You're not going to die, you silly woman. If you'd only keep to your diet properly, you'd be as right as rain in six months.'

'Promise?'

'I promise. And now stop being so neurotic,' he said briskly, 'and let's have lunch. I have to go out again in half an hour, and I'd like something to eat first.'

★ ★ ★

Dr. Mansbridge saw Catherine waiting at the bottom of Elm Walk, slowed down, and opened the car door further.

Like many people with dull or frustrated lives, Catherine seldom felt wholly well. She had never bothered to take these pains, this lassitude, to Dr. Horace's surgery; she had simply gone doggedly on day after day, 'working them off', as they say; but with Dr. Mansbridge to consult, it became a very different matter. Each separate little trivial complaint was an excuse for seeing him.

Dr. Mansbridge was conscientious. He did not allow his patients' neurotic tendencies to blind him to the validity of their physical complaints. He recognized that Miss Duncton was one of these pathetic cases for whom little could be done until the tyrannical old father's death set her free. Meanwhile, he pursued the clues he noticed in her fingernails, her lips, the too-white skin over her cheekbones.

She could not hide her dismay when he told her that she was to go once a week to the General Hospital at Cambury for treatment. That was not what she wanted at all. That would ruin everything for her.

It would take away all excuse for seeing him. She protested that it was impossible for her to leave her father for so long. She was filled with horror at the thought of the interminable bus journeys, the hanging about, the hopeless complications of trying to find a friend who would sit with her father the while. But her obstinacy only made Dr. Mansbridge impatient.

'You see, Father doesn't like me to go out,' she murmured timidly.

'This is not for pleasure. You must explain to your father — or I will, if you prefer — ' ('Oh, no, thank you.' She clasped her hands fervently.) ' — that you have a serious blood condition which must be checked. It is essential for you to have this treatment now; once the condition is aggravated, it will be much harder to cure. You might even have to become an inpatient.'

'How could I do that? There's no one else to look after Father.'

'Well, if you're sensible, you'll see to it that it doesn't become necessary.' But she was silly and stubborn: he could not alarm her, and it was useless to reason with her, for she could not understand reason. He knew she would do nothing about it. But it bothered him; he was too conscientious to leave it at that. He frowned. At last, rather crossly, he said he would arrange to take her in to Cambury himself.

The silly blissful smile on her face made her father ask irritably what she was grinning at like a village idiot; but even his acerbity could not quench her happiness. The weekly drives stood out as bright as beacons against Catherine's colourless days. Why they meant so much to her, it would be hard to explain to anyone who has never been love-obsessed. Often he scarcely spoke; but she was content in his presence, his nearness. She could hardly have asked more. It was enough to sit, as she sat now, watching with passionate attention the movements of his hands, loose and confident, on the wheel.

The thumb of his hogskin glove was still split; she had noticed the tear last week. She stroked up a savage black mark against that wife of his in her mind. *She* obviously did not care tuppence about him, not even enough to keep his appearance decently respectable. How could he care for a woman who neglected him so shamefully? Catherine wondered if she would dare bring her little huswif next week as if by chance, and find some excuse to mend it for him. Then he might see that not all women were like his wife; perhaps he would ponder how different his life might have been if he had married someone like her ... It made her heart thump in her side to think of doing some small service for him: she longed to please him, to do anything for him: she longed more than anything for him to look at her just once as if he really saw her.

Puffy grey eiderdowns smothered the sun, and by the time Catherine left the hospital it had begun to rain. She went into the teashop down the street to wait for him, and ordered a cup of tea, but before she had time to drink it, the doctor came in and she quickly got up.

'No,' he said cheerfully, 'sit down. I'll have a cup with you. As a matter of fact, I'll have something to eat.' He picked up the menu. 'I'm hungry. You know what Monday dinner is,' he said with a laughing grimace.

She was shocked. Genuinely. So that woman, his wife, didn't even feed him properly, which everyone knew to be the unforgivable sin. It made Catherine's heart burn within her for pity, watching him eat the poached eggs on toast. Neglected and hungry, perhaps he was lonely too, underneath his calm and capable exterior. Who could tell what another person was feeling? One could be hungry and neglected spiritually as well as materially, and that perhaps was worse. If only she could tell him that she too was starving and there was no one to care for her either.

(Old Miss Lucas said to Miss Barnaby the next day, 'My dear, they were so taken up with one another they never even noticed me in my little corner. She couldn't take her eyes off him. I must say, I was astonished, I always thought he was such a nice man, so devoted to his wife.'

'Oh, I'm sure he is,' said Miss Barnaby.

'You wouldn't have thought so to see those two together, believe me. Laughing as though they'd neither of them a care in the world.'

'Laughing? Of course, we all know the doctor has quite a way with him, very jolly and all that, but Catherine has always seemed such a quiet girl.'

'It is always the quiet ones, isn't it? Poor Mrs. Mansbridge!')

As they drove homewards through the slanting drizzle, Dr. Mansbridge suddenly remarked, 'Oh, by the way, I'm afraid I shan't be able to take you in next week. It's the day my locum arrives, and I shall have to be there to meet him. There'll be a great deal to attend to before I go away.'

'You're going away?' she said with a sinking heart.

'Yes, I'm off the week after next on my holiday.'

'Oh,' she said. And the day which had been bright with silver rain suddenly became desolate and blank. 'How lovely! Where are you going?'

'Cornwall. A little village about ten miles from Falmouth, where there is nothing to do all day but fish.'

'You like fishing?'

'There's nothing in the world I like better,' he said. 'My idea of heaven.' He made a wry grimace. 'Ah, if I were only free!' he sighed.

She heard his words between pain and triumph. A pulse beat thickly in her throat.

It pained her to realize that she knew nothing of his pleasures, that all his private life was hidden from her; it was as if he had shut a door in her face. At the same time, another and more secret door had been opened with his cry for freedom. To her, the words were a confession that he did not care for his wife any longer — a triumphant vindication of her innermost conviction. She stared down at her hands to hide her face from him. She dared not let him see she understood.

He pulled out to pass a car ambling along on the crown of the road. ('Fool!' he yelled.) He turned a swift glance at her. 'I hope you're not going to let me down, after all the trouble they've taken over your case at the C.G.H. You will go to your treatments just the same, won't you? They're very pleased with your progress, but it would be criminally foolish to stop now when your case is just on the turn.'

'Shall you be in Cornwall long, then?'

'Only a fortnight, I'm sorry to say. I promised my wife a fortnight in Portugal afterwards. It will be our first holiday abroad since before the war, and she's looking forward to it almost as keenly as I'm looking forward to Cornwall.'

But all Catherine could grasp was that he would be away a month. Five weeks, counting the week she would not see him. She stared out at the dumb dejected cows looming at them as they passed. She wondered how she would live without these excursions to look forward to each week; this was probably the last time she would be alone with him. A groan involuntarily escaped her.

'I beg your pardon?' he said, inclining his head slightly towards her.

'I was just thinking that by the time you return, my treatment may be finished.'

'Well, we'll certainly hope so,' he said cheerily, and from his tone one might have supposed he was *glad* these tiresome expeditions were coming to an end.

She was too crushed to speak again, and they drove on in silence until he drew up outside her home. With her hand on the car door, she said desperately, 'Shall I see you at the fete next week?'

'What fete is that?' he said vaguely.

She said eagerly, 'It's in aid of the Dr.

Barnardo Homes. Do come. We need as many people as we can get. I shall be at the Home-Made Sweets stall. Tell me what your favourite sweet is, and I'll make some specially for you,' she urged with pathetic ardour.

He laughed.

'I don't eat sweets, Miss Duncton.' And then, seeing her face fall like a disappointed child's, he said, as he would have to a child, 'Never mind, I'll buy some for my wife,' jollying her along.

She turned away her head so that he should not see her lip so foolishly trembling. She clung a moment longer to the chromium handle.

'Will you really?' she said at last.

'Of course.'

'Then I shall look out for you.' Her shy glance wavered towards him. 'That's a promise, isn't it?' she said huskily and hurried away with beating heart.

She hastened up the path. Her father rapped on the pane. She looked up, a smile on her face.

★　★　★

As the car hissed past Mr. and Mrs. Ambrose walking their dogs in the rain, Mrs. Ambrose had said:

'There goes poor Robert and that dreary Duncton girl. I'm frankly surprised that he can't find himself someone better than that to amuse himself with.'

'How do you know he *is* amusing himself with her?' Mr. Ambrose idly inquired, slashing at the bracken with his walking-stick (bracken was a pest and must be kept down).

A retriever scooted past them into the thicket with something dark and bloodsome hanging from its jaws.

Mrs. Ambrose shouted after him, frenziedly whacking her raincoat.

'Basil! Bas-il! Here! Drop it, you filthy brute!' But she called in vain. 'Damn that dog! Now he'll be sick all night!' she prophesied gloomily. 'What were we saying …? Oh, my dear, I thought you knew. Everyone's talking about it. Not that I pay any attention to gossip. And frankly, even if it's true that he takes her to a hotel in Cambury, I'd be the last person to condemn him. Only I do rather deplore his taste.

And, fond as I am of poor old Robert, I do honestly think he ought to be a bit more discreet in his conduct. I've an idea that even Mrs. M. knows about it: she's been looking ghastly lately.'

'They say she's ill.'

'Enough to make any woman ill if she's grieving over her husband's blatant infidelities. I'm afraid one has always taken it for granted that she didn't care tuppence about him. It's rather too bad of Robert.'

'Oh, come! 'Blatant infidelity' is surely a bit steep, dear.'

'Isn't it blatant when it becomes a matter for common gossip?'

'I dare say the whole thing has been grossly exaggerated. Holding hands and a muffed kiss or two, is my guess. I can't see Robert going off the deep end; and as for the Duncton miss, she doesn't look as if she could say boo to a goose, much less take another woman's husband away from her.'

Mrs. Ambrose, knowing her sex rather better than he did, merely smiled a sardonic smile.

'Dumbo!' yelled Mr. Ambrose suddenly. *'Dumbo,* damn you! Oh, curse that animal!

What, dear?'

'I only wondered how it was all going to end.'

'With a bang, you mean, or a whimper?' said Mr. Ambrose neatly.

3

Loneliness Seeps In With the Silence

Seizing a moment when the shop was empty, Naomi slipped through the back to pop the joint into the oven when she heard Crispin laugh: a low, fond chuckle that made Naomi freeze. The sound came from the queer little room she used as an office. Crispin was supposed to be upstairs in her studio, working. She knew Naomi hated her to use the telephone for merely private conversations during shop hours, and she must have been talking there for at least half an hour, Naomi calculated. She would be talking to 'that woman', of course. At the sound of the soft, throaty laugh, a sort of trembling rage came over Naomi. She was about to put her head round the open door and coldly inquire just how much longer Crispin intended to be, when she heard her protest laughingly, 'Oh, darling, really you mustn't say that,' and at the same moment the office door, with quiet effrontery, swung slowly shut in Naomi's face. She flushed to the roots of her hair and, biting her lip, walked quickly away.

* * *

Harry let himself into the old stone house with silent assurance, soundlessly turning handles to peer into rooms, padding in those dirty plimsolls of his as quietly as a cat. Editha never heard him enter her bedroom as she stood there with her back to him, talking on the telephone, leaning negligently against the wall. He stood there listening with his arms folded.

It was less that mysterious sense that makes one aware of not being alone than the foul reek of his pipe that made Editha turn. She gave a shriek; cried 'Damn!' and then quickly put down the receiver.

She collected herself magnificently, though her face was white. She said in her sharp, hectoring way:

'How dare you come in here like that! What do you mean by it?'

He surveyed her calmly, one might almost say critically. He did not trouble to reply.

She said furiously:

'How did you get in?'

He raised one eyebrow.

Politely removing his pipe, he said:

'Through the door.'

'I thought I'd made it clear that I wouldn't have you hanging round the place where I happen to live. You've all the rest of England to choose from; there's no need to make a nuisance of yourself here.' He didn't answer. 'I won't have it. Do you hear me?'

'Of course I hear you. I should think they could hear you down the street.'

She knew this side of Harry, and feared it. The sunny geniality of the other day had vanished; he was in one of his dangerous moods.

She began again firmly:

'Harry, I forbid — '

He cut in coolly:

'I shall stay where it suits me. It's a free country. Where did you really think I would go? How far did you imagine I could get, on your generous half-quid? Use your loaf, my good girl!'

'If you have come here to beg for money again, you might as well go now. Once and for all, I — will — not — give — you — a — penny,' she said, stamping a foot.

He shrugged indifferently.

'As it happens, that is not why I am here.'

'Well, what is it this time?' she said impatiently, like the fairy fish to the fisherman.

'That suit of Robert's you promised me.'

'Nothing was said about a suit. I told you I'd try to find some socks and a shirt. I also said I'd send them on to you when you gave me an address.'

'You can see I must have a suit. And a decent pair of shoes. I can't go around like this.'

'Well, I can't do anything now; I haven't the time.'

'I'll wait,' he said, folding his arms again.

'I tell you I haven't the time now. I'll send them on later.'

'I'll wait,' he repeated.

'Leave me alone, Harry,' she complained, angry tears coming to her eyes. 'I won't be badgered.'

He began to whistle softly between his teeth 'Brother Mine and Sister Mine' from *Die Fledermaus,* a tune that had been their private signal as children. Now it was an ominous hint.

She said bitterly, 'You use our relationship to blackmail me. Have you no conscience?'

'Have *you* no conscience? When you eat your three good meals and sleep peacefully in your comfortable warm bed, do you never think of your only brother, homeless and penniless, often hungry, often with no roof to sleep under? Have you no conscience?' he repeated.

She dropped wearily onto the edge of the bed.

'It's not fair!' she complained. 'Whatever your misfortunes are, they're your own fault, not mine. It's no good trying to make me feel responsible. I've troubles enough of my own, believe me. I'm a sick woman. I shouldn't be worried. If you want to know the truth, I'm dying.'

'So are we all. That's the condition of mankind.'

'I mean it, Harry. In a few months I shall

be dead.'

'I hope that will be to my advantage. You'll have left your only brother something, I trust.'

She gazed at him with loathing, really hurt by his brutal cynicism.

'So much for your brotherly feeling! All you care about is whether you will benefit by my death.'

'You expect me to feel pity for you, when you feel none for me,' he said lightly.

★　★　★

Betsy Golding came out of the school office and glanced through the mullioned window at the courtyard below. In a shadowed archway opposite, two dark forms could be discerned. The taller, she could tell by his shoulders and the turn of his head in silhouette against the sunlight beyond, was Edward. And the other, taking little rocking twirling steps to and fro as she talked, like a courting bird, was unmistakably Janet. She moved from the shadows into the brilliant courtyard, a lithe figure in her emerald dress, her wide scarlet mouth laughing up at him. He took a step towards her, and she pushed him away with a hand on his arm, shaking her head so that the long black hair swung out. Laughing, he caught a great handful and gave it a friendly tug. For just a moment their eyes met and they held each other's gaze; and then Janet, with a laugh, ran lightly across the courtyard, and Edward turned on his heel and disappeared through the dark archway.

Mrs. Golding went out into the sunlit street, past the peony-bright cottage gardens, to the house where they lodged, which had seemed like Paradise to her till this moment. Now it was just an ugly little house that stared back at her from unfriendly windows.

The trifling episode she had witnessed assumed the spiteful proportions of an evil dream. She had somehow the ridiculous but painful notion that Edward didn't love her, had never loved her. What chiefly exercised her now was what she was to do, how she was to behave. Theoretically, she understood all the secret lore of wifehood: she knew she must be patient, loving, silent, and above all unreproachful. It was fatal, she knew, to nag and question; that would only send him flying guiltily out of the house and to the other woman's arms for comfort. Some wives, she knew, created towering scenes that terrorized their husbands into meek behaviour. But that was a role Betsy would never attempt: she was too proud, too civilized, to fight. Her role was the discretion of Scheherazade; he should never know she knew.

Her smile felt stiff on her cheeks as she served the cottage pie and rattled out the sort of remarks she was accustomed to amuse him with at meals. Mr. Golding, immersed in his papers, responded with grunts. Once term had begun, he had taken on this maddening habit of reading with his meals — she always tried not to mind, she *wanted* him to do what he wanted to do — but today his stolid inattention was agony to her. And the food churned round in her mouth and would not be swallowed: tears were closing her throat.

She put down her fork. To her own consternation, she heard herself say:

'What a pity you didn't marry Janet after all, when you're so fond of one another.'

79

'What?' he said, vaguely. And after a moment he raised his eyes from the page to give her a long stare. 'We're surely not starting that all over again, are we?' he asked plaintively.

If she had been clever, she could have withdrawn the attack; there was still time to laugh it off. But something in his tone, some half-concealed contempt she fancied she heard in his words, made it imperative for her to prick back. She simply could not help herself saying:

'Everyone knows you're mad about her.'

Mr. Golding pushed away his plate and leaned back in his chair with a resigned expression. He said, with that deliberate patience that is so much more exacerbating than downright irritation:

'Now, then, what is this all about? I'd like to get to the bottom of it once and for all, if you don't mind. I see what a fool I was ever to tell you I'd had anything to do with the damned girl.'

'It wouldn't have made any difference. It was only a question of time before I learnt the truth. One has only to see you both together when you think you're unobserved,' she said with a shaky laugh.

'May one ask what you mean by that remark?' Edward asked with alarming frigidity.

It frightened her to see him so severe and inimical. In their inevitable love-quarrels he had only stormed and flung about: there had never been this icy disapproval, as though he hated her; as though he saw right through her to her small, mean soul, and was sickened by it. She defended herself in attack, saying aggressively:

'I saw you with her under Boulter's Arch today.'

'Well? What was it you saw?'

Her voice wavered humiliatingly as she said, 'You couldn't keep your hands off her ... It was revolting ... Horrible ... And she was *gazing* up at you as if ... ' Her voice quavered to an end and she clapped a handkerchief to her eyes. Her chair fell over as she sprang up.

He halted her at the door with his authoritative schoolmaster's voice.

'One moment, please, Betsy!'

Still clutching the door handle, she turned and faced him blindly, her great eyes glittering with unshed tears.

'If it's all the same to you, I must insist on getting this idiotic business cleared up. A man in my position can't afford to be made to look ridiculous by his wife following him about to spy and make scenes — '

'I wasn't spying!' burst from her lips in a wild indignant cry. 'I just happened to see you as I was passing.'

Ignoring her interruption as if unheard, he continued coldly: 'If you elect to chivvy me in the privacy of our home, that's one thing; I can put up with it. But I must seriously insist that you do not conduct yourself so that it becomes a public affair.'

'It's you who've done that,' she said with a bitter little smile.

'You wilfully misunderstand me. All I am asking is that you refrain from discussing this vulgar obsession of yours with all and sundry.'

'I never have,' she cried. 'My God, you're unfair! I've never spoken of it to a soul,' she repeated, dashing a hand across her eyes like a child.

'I simply refer you to your own words a few minutes ago. Are you telling me that my ears deceived me, that I never heard you say everyone knew I was crazy over her?'

'I said I hadn't spoken about it to anyone: that doesn't mean that other people don't speak of it to me. People are sorry for me, you see. It's charming for me to see the pity in their eyes. Why, I'd hardly set foot in this place when I was told about it by a complete stranger, someone quite outside school life. So you see, it was common gossip before ever I came. And if you don't believe me, it was Mrs. Mansbridge, the doctor's wife.'

'That foul old busybody!' he exclaimed irately, kicking the table. 'I'd like to cut her throat!'

'Because it was from her I learnt the truth? I suppose you imagine that otherwise I might never have found out, and you could have gone on deceiving me.'

'I've not been deceiving you, you little idiot!' Edward shouted, suddenly at the end of his patience.

'If you're not, you'd like to; it comes to the same thing. I saw the way you looked, the way you kept touching one another.'

He seized her by the shoulders and shook her.

'For God's sake, stop it, Betsy! You're building up a great mountain of nonsense in your mind that you'll end by believing. You know there's not a word of truth in all this.'

She did know it, but she couldn't bring herself to believe it.

'Look how it excites you even to talk about it,' she said with a wincing smile, tormenting herself more than him.

'Oh, dear God!' he snapped.

The clock striking in the corner made him glance at his watch.

'I must go,' he said. 'I'll be late.' He took hold of her cool, fresh upper arms and drew her towards him. His voice softened. 'Give me a kiss, Bets, and stop being such a goose.'

But it was no use; she couldn't respond to him, she simply couldn't recover as quickly at that. Her dignity, her pride, her confidence in their mutual love and understanding were too injured. She longed more than anything to feel the comfort of his arms about her once again, she longed to weep out her misery and humiliation on his breast ... but somehow, until he apologized, it was impossible. Until he apologized, she could not ask him to forgive *her,* and only mutual forgiveness could salve this hideous wound to their love. Her stupid mind betrayed her heart. She stiffened obstinately in his grasp and pulled away.

'Oh, damn that infernal woman!' cried Mr. Golding, striding from the room.

★　★　★

'Cavee, you ass!' hissed young Gosse, tactfully kicking Boddy minor on the ankle. 'The Goldbug isn't half laying it on this apres-midi; he's in a stinking bate.'

★　★　★

In Robert's well-cut suit and chestnut-polished shoes, Harry looked a different character altogether, as clean-run as an English Gentleman in a snob advertisement; there was even a certain romantic charm about those bloodshot eyes and tarnished hair.

Mind you, though most of his time was spent idling in pubs, he wasn't idle. He was engaged in Market Research. That is to say, he was looking for the right mug. In a small place like this, one could not afford to make mistakes, one did not get a second chance.

In the meantime, he had a fund of jolly little tricks and problems to pose to his bar-cronies; they could always be persuaded to bet a few shillings on the answer to how many buttons there were on a chap's suit, or a four-letter word ending in 'ENY', or some complicated arrangement of matches or coins. Harry picked up a lot of useful information that way as well as cash.

He had his eye on a jaunty little woman who always came in alone. She looked the right sort, a sporty (not sporting) type. A widow, they said. She wore her dusty fawn hair loose to her shoulders in an out-of-date style that was a little too youthful to be quite becoming. Usually a scarlet coat was slung over her shoulders, with a chiffon handkerchief to match knotted round one wrist. Bracelets tinkled with every movement. A thin wool jersey hugged her breasts, and her little round behind wagged in butcher-blue jeans the colour of her eyes — eyes which became as bright as glass as the evening wore on ... and as the drinks went down. Harry could see she was lonely.

He strolled casually across and bought her a drink.

* * *

Most evenings, Mrs. Petrie strolled up to The George. There was really nothing else to do. She could not stand too much of her own company. Particularly after dark, it got on her nerves. The radio which had jazzed out all day suddenly became intolerable at nightfall; yet, once it was switched off, loneliness seeped in with the silence.

She lived in a tiny, dolled-up cottage with trees in tubs outside the door, like an illustration in a children's book. It had been their weekend cottage when she was married. She had chanced to be down there when she got the letter from her husband to say he had left her; and, having nowhere else to go, she had simply stayed on there.

It was four years ago since her husband had run off with some little trollop of a girl. In time, Mrs. Petrie would probably have got around to divorcing Mr. Petrie; but before that could happen, he and the other woman were involved in a motor smash and he was killed outright. Luckily for Mrs. Petrie, he had never made a will, so such estate as there was came to her: not a great deal, but enough. Though it might have been happier for her if she had been obliged to work, for there seemed nothing to do with her life now. It had fallen to pieces and she did not know how to put it together again. She was not the sort of woman who knows how to live alone. She was just one of the many little girls who grew old without ever growing up.

Despite the shock to her self-esteem, while Nicholas was still alive, she had kidded herself with the absurd unnourished Penelope-myth that one day he would return and all would be as it was before. But once he was dead, there was not even a myth for her to live by — there was nothing left at all.

Not that their marriage had been a great impassioned love-affair; they had fought and been as unhappy as most other couples. Yet now she missed it terribly, and could not even tell exactly what it was she missed. The gay little pub crawls, the occasional mad sprees, the weekend parties with their friends were all gone for ever. For no one, she had painfully to learn, is interested in a woman on her own. Particularly a woman no longer young. A woman who had failed. She was constantly aware of this sense of failure. Her husband's defection had undermined her confidence in her powers as a woman to attract and hold a man (and to the kind of woman Mrs. Petrie was, there is nothing else that matters).

She craved companionship and affection. She needed to be needed. Occasionally, sickened by her uselessness, she would get a job in some craft shop where they were used to untrained people, or try her hand at something 'artistic', making 'amusing little lampshades' or 'clever' costume jewellery out of painted shells. But nothing that wasn't human held her attention for long: she was too scatter brained and frivolous.

Mrs. Petrie found Harry amusing. She became very gay, and heard herself laughing a shade too loudly at his jokes. At closing time, he walked her back to her cottage in the pale twilight. She was surprised by a flutter at her heart when he dropped a kiss gently on her mouth, and for a moment her mouth clung to his.

'You sweet thing, you,' he murmured.

He so obviously expected to be asked in that it would have been ungracious not to. 'What are you doing?' she protested weakly when he took her in his arms. 'You mustn't,' she said with a helpless laugh. 'No, really ... '

Darkness crept softly through the windows and loitered in the corners, listening to the murmurs that broke the silence from time to time.

★   ★   ★

For all her pretended bohemianism, the thought that he might take her lightly filled her with horror.

'I don't know what you must think of me,' she whispered, with her face close to his.

'I think you're a darling.'

'You mustn't think I always behave like this.' She gave a faint nervous laugh. 'I'd be too scared, for one thing. How could one know one wouldn't get one's throat cut, or find oneself in the clutches of a crook, or something?'

'Oh, thanks,' he said.

'Silly, not you! I knew *you* were all right.' She stroked the end of his loosened tie. 'You see, it was the first thing I noticed about you when you came over to speak to me. Nick was a Wykehamist.'

'Nick?' he said. 'A Wykehamist?' He hadn't a notion what she was talking about.

'My husband. That was how I recognized your old Winchester tie.'

He inspected Robert's tie curiously by the dim glow of the electric fire.

'The Old School Tie, God bless it! I always say you never know when it will be useful,' he said blithely.

* * *

To have a lover was for Mrs. Petrie like waking to life again after the deep deadness of the last years. The fountain of gladness in her heart continually flung up little sprays of gratitude. She was in love — or believed she was, which comes to much the same thing. He came to seem everything she most admired in a man: he had looks and charm and gaiety and an undefeatable courage; he was resolutely humorous even about

91

his disastrous financial state, for he did not attempt to conceal from her that he was flat broke. Of course, he tried for jobs, but for a man of his age employment was hard to find. What one needed was a bit of capital.

'God, if I had some of the money I've chucked away in my time!' he sighed. 'I'd know what to do with it now, all right.'

'What?'

'One learns too late, alas. I'd put it into some safe and steady little business. Like a brothel.'

She burst out laughing: it was so unexpected, so ludicrous, so typical of his whimsical humour. He looked at her in surprise and then joined in her merriment, pleased that she should be amused by it.

Mrs. Petrie was entranced by her vision of lush pink rooms with girls in chemises and an electric piano in the parlour — an idea she'd culled from a picture she'd once seen.

'You kid,' he laughed, 'I hate to disillusion you, but that's not what I have in mind at all. Nothing so crude. I only want what is called a house of assignation. You see ...' he began, and she listened with amusement to his absorbed explanation of costs and profits. The subject evidently fascinated him, and it became a sort of joke between them, the idiotic kind of joke lovers delight to share, part of the fantasy of their lives.

Most days, he went off to one of the big neighbouring towns — to 'see what was doing', as he put it. And Mrs. Petrie drifted about her little cottage all day in a happy dream, waiting for him to return. Their cosy, unreal existence seemed almost too good to be true, and sometimes she caught her breath in uneasy dread that somehow it must come to an end.

What did happen was that one day Harry took her in to Lowbridge with him, and with an air of superb extravagance stood her lunch at The Market Hotel. Flushed with wine, she giggled happily at the absurdities he invented about the other diners. In the corner behind them, Lucien Verney, with his customary 'pot' and 'plate', held the newspaper well before his face so as not to be observed. The meal spun out, and they had nearly finished when a man came in whom Harry recognized with a loud cry. He came over, and Harry insisted on his joining them.

'Meet the wife,' he said, pinching Mrs. Petrie's elbow fondly.

Harry's friend was a fattish, middle-aged man with a leery eye. He greeted her with polite indifference and immediately plunged into man-talk with Harry to which she only half-attended. This boring encounter was spoiling their delightful outing, was all she thought. But Harry noticed everything, and even though he wasn't looking at her, he seemed aware of her dull face; for he suddenly leaned towards her and, squeezing her hand, gave her an intimate smile and mysteriously said:

'He's got a flat.'

'How nice,' said Mrs. Petrie, with a vague smile at Harry's friend.

'Just what we've been looking for,' Harry confided with half-closed eyes.

'You couldn't do better; take my word, little lady,' said Harry's friend.

What on earth was he talking about? Mrs. Petrie wondered. Was this one of Harry's elaborate jokes?

'The refs were okay,' the fat man was saying, 'so I brought the agreement along.

If you'd like to have a dekko.' He took some papers out of his briefcase and passed them across to Harry.

'It'll have to be in my wife's name,' Harry said, flipping over the pages as he scanned them. 'That's all right with you, dear, isn't it?' he added casually, turning to her.

'Yes, of course,' she said uncertainly, still not seeing what it was about.

'You sign here, dear ... and here ... ' He pointed out the places to her, laying the papers before her and flattening them with his hand. The fat man unscrewed a fountain pen and passed it to her politely.

She looked from one to the other in bewilderment.

'What do you want me to do?'

'Just sign the agreement, dear, that's all.'

'But what for? I don't understand.'

'It's for the flat, dear. The flat we've been looking for,' Harry explained, with the merest suggestion of impatience in his voice.

He looked quite serious, there was nothing about his expression to indicate a joke, and to her bewilderment was added a faint alarm.

'I don't understand,' she said again.

'Oh, good Lord!' he exclaimed, setting his lips.

'Harry,' she said in a low, pleading voice, 'I want to speak to you.'

The two men exchanged a glance.

The fat man said, with heavy tact, 'Look, I've got to make a couple of phone calls, if you'll excuse me,' and waddled away.

'Now what are you baulking at?' Harry asked in displeasure.

'But, Harry, I honestly don't know what it's all about. You never told me.'

'Never told you?' he repeated, amazed. 'Why, we've been into it again and again. What sort of gag are you pulling now?'

'But Harry, you can't mean … ' She gave a nervous laugh. 'Is it a joke, then?'

'A joke? I don't know what you're driving at. We've been over the whole damned project time and time again; you never pretended it was a joke before. You were as keen on the idea as I was. You never raised any objections then, so why all this fuss suddenly?'

She stared at him incredulously.

'One of us is crazy,' she muttered. 'It was only a game. You must know it was only a game. How could you have dreamed that I would really do anything like that? You must have a horrible opinion of me.' She stared down at the white tablecloth shimmering before her eyes. 'I suppose I've only myself to thank for that.'

'Well, my God, this is a fine time to back out, letting me down at the last moment,' he said savagely. 'After all the trouble I've been to. Making a chap look a perfect fool.'

She pleated the cloth in careful folds.

'If this thing means so much to you, why not sign the agreement yourself?'

'Because I can't, of course. Why do you suppose I had to give your bank for a reference? I'm an undischarged bankrupt.'

'I didn't know,' she muttered, sick at heart at this sudden revelation of his careful secret plotting behind her back. She said huskily, 'I thought you really were fond of me. I thought you meant all the things you said. What a fool I've been!'

'No, my dear, I've been the fool,' Harry said with a bitter laugh. 'I imagined that in you, I'd found the woman I'd been looking for all my life: a partner, a real sport. One more illusion vanished.' He made a conjuror's gesture in the air. 'God, how you pulled the wool over my eyes! I trusted you!'

It was astonishing how he contrived to make her feel the one in the wrong, the one who had let him down, so subtly did he turn the tables on her. Thoroughly muddled with wine and shock and his queerly theatrical air of disillusion, she struggled confusedly with the feelings of guilt and bewilderment creeping over her. She leant her head on her hand.

'But why didn't you tell me all this before? If you really believed I'd agree to it, why did you have to hide from me that you were using my bank for a reference? It was because you knew it was illegal, and you must have known I'd never do anything illegal,' she pondered aloud.

He said contemptuously, 'You'd never do anything illegal! Excuse my smile! Never bought anything on the black market during the war? Never fiddled your income tax returns?'

She turned away from his angry blood-shot eyes.

'That's different. Everyone does those

things.'

'Oh, if everybody breaks the law, that's all right, is it? You're cheating, you're actually depriving other people; but what harm would I be doing, pray? I'm not *forcing* anyone to use my house. It's simply there for their convenience. Has it ever occurred to you that there are hundreds of people in love who literally haven't anywhere to go where they can be alone together? Not everyone is as lucky as we — as we were,' he amended.

She was silent.

A waiter presented the bill.

'Well, that's that!' he said, when the waiter had gone. 'You'd better cut off now.'

'Aren't you coming?' she timidly asked.

'No. What's the use? In any case, I'll have to stay and cook up some story for this chap when he comes back.'

'I'm sorry.'

'Oh, I'll get over it. I've had worse disappointments than this in my day. I'll move on, try my luck elsewhere.'

'How do you mean?'

'Oh, don't be so simple! I've got to make money somehow. If I can't make it here, I must go somewhere where I can. I have my own sense of honour, you know, and one thing I'll never do is to sponge off a woman.'

'Are you trying to tell me this is the end?' She was white to the lips.

'I should have thought that was evident.'

'But Harry, please, we — I can't let you go like this,' she quavered desperately.

'Don't let's have a scene, my dear. It would be too ugly. Let's just acknowledge that it didn't work out the way we hoped, and say goodbye without ill will.'

'Harry, I can't say goodbye here, like this. For God's sake, come back this evening and let us talk this thing over!'

'No sense in prolonging the agony. My motto has always been, cut your losses quick.'

'But, Harry, I love you,' she whispered hoarsely.

He smiled grimly at that and stood up.

'Let's clear out, shall we?' he said politely. Blindly, she followed him to the hotel entrance, and on the steps outside he said in the same cool tone, 'You can find your way home, can't you?' and turned back to the hotel.

'Harry!' she cried. But he never looked round.

Lucien, on his way back to the office, saw her moving like a somnambulist through the buffeting crowds with the tears still running down her cheeks.

4

Slender Girls in Summer Dresses

'Had a good day?' Mrs. Verney asked her son, as she asked every evening, having no suspicion how the question maddened him.

He mumbled a nothing as usual, and went to wash. Presently, when he came to the table, the next question arrived: 'Anything interesting happened today?'

To that also, there could never be an answer. What did she suppose could happen of interest in a dreary provincial architect's drawing-office? The petty details of his day would be as tedious to relate as they were to endure.

Mrs. Verney brought in the big dish on which the food was arranged in an exquisite pattern of colour (she liked her food to look romantic besides tasting well) and began to serve it. That was always the moment for the third question: 'Did you see anyone we know in Lowbridge?'

Tensed to receive it, he found himself growling out 'No' before he could stop himself. He had to fight a silent battle with his will before he could bring himself to mutter, without any of the gaiety he had originally intended, 'Only Mrs. Petrie.'

'Oh, really, darling? What was she doing?'

'Sobbing her eyes out in Market High Street,' Lucien said, doing his best.

'No!' said his mother. 'How extraordinary! Why, do you suppose?'

He had savoured the incident keenly himself and with (for him) a surprising curiosity that had made him look forward quite eagerly to discussing it with his mother, for once in a way; but now to his dismay, the avid glint in her eye revolted him. Having begun, however, there could be no turning back till the end. He sighed, and began flatly to recount what he had seen.

★   ★   ★

Lately, Mr. Duncton had become more irascible than ever. He did not sleep at night, he said. He complained that the sleeping pills prescribed by Dr. Horace did no good, had

103

lost their effect. And Catherine, his obstinate cruel Goneril, was making an absurd issue of asking the doctor to call and prescribe him something stronger. She had the gall to tell him that she could not ask the doctor to come out for something so trivial as a sleepless night, and anyway she was convinced that he would never give her father a stronger drug; those barbiturates, he had warned her, were dangerous. There was no doing anything with the girl! When he suggested increasing the dose, she pretended to be horrified.

'Father, you might never wake up again!' she cried.

'So much the better. Who would care if I never woke again? Not I! And certainly not you, my Goneril.'

In silence she folded back the sheet.

'Perhaps you'll sleep better tonight, Father,' she said in a soothing voice.

'Does it please you to watch me die by inches of pain and exhaustion? Does keeping me alive, however painfully, salve your miserable conscience? A good daughter! So people tell me. How lucky I am, they say, to have such a good child. It's ironical to think it isn't me they pity, but you.

Doubtless, Goneril too went about piously complaining how hard life was for her with her intolerable old father.'

'Father, I never say such things!'

'It is all the more effective if it is not put into words.'

'I never think them, either,' she protested.

'Ah, the monstrous nature of the female! She has her own subtle methods of tormenting a helpless creature utterly in her power. One would suppose that in my own home I might expect some small kindness, some small consideration from my only child. If the truth were known, I'd be better treated in a public institution.'

'Yes, Father,' Catherine said meekly, knowing it was useless to argue when he was in this frame of mind.

He uttered a sound that represented laughter.

'Yes, I thought you would agree with that. You'd like that, wouldn't you? Bury the old man out of sight somewhere while he is still alive and forget him!'

Catherine bent to straighten the bedclothes, and it gratified him to see that her lips were trembling.

It was not out of malice that Mrs. Verney called at Lavender Cottage the next day. Her feeble pretext was to ask if Mrs. Petrie would help with the refreshments at the next Conservative dance.

The disorder of the little sitting-room, with its rumpled cushions and cigarette ends littered about, conjured to her imagination the picture of someone smoking furiously as she restlessly paced the floor, every now and then flinging herself on to the cushions to weep.

Mrs. Petrie was abstracted, so far away with her unhappy thoughts, that she scarcely attended to what Mrs. Verney was saying. Her face was white, puffy, tragic between the soft fall of her faded little-girl hair. Mrs. Verney's sympathy could scarcely contain itself, and she was about to break the silence with some impulsive gesture when the cottage door — leading straight into the parlour, as they always did — opened.

Mrs. Petrie, startled, cried out, 'Harry!' to the figure standing there.

He looked at her solemnly without a

word. Mrs. Verney got up to go, murmuring vague excuses. They listened in silence to her heels tapping down the path.

'Why have you come back?' Mrs. Petrie said at last.

'To collect my bits.'

'Go ahead. They're upstairs,' she said, turning her back and pretending to rummage in a drawer.

In a few moments he came down again.

'Could I trouble you for a piece of brown paper?'

'You'll find some in the kitchen,' she said indifferently.

Neither looked at the other as he passed through the living-room. Presently she called, 'Can't you find it?' He muttered something she did not catch and she went to the kitchen. 'There,' she said coolly, laying her hand on it at once and pulling out a sheet.

She found herself suddenly face to face with him. Their eyes met, and for a long moment they gazed at one another. The paper in her hand shook. 'Oh, Harry,' she muttered and flung herself against him.

'There, there, Toots,' he murmured,

stroking her hair.

'I've been so miserable,' she wept into his shoulder.

'You mustn't cry,' he said softly.

'I thought I was never going to see you again. You said such cruel things.'

'Have you forgiven me?'

'Can you ever forgive me?'

'What for?'

'Letting you down like that.'

'My fault,' he said gallantly. 'It was a misunderstanding, that's all.'

'It's generous of you to say that, Harry, but I reproach myself. I couldn't sleep last night, thinking about it.'

'You poor sweet! That's why I came back. I couldn't go away without seeing that you were all right.'

'You won't go now,' she murmured, her cheek against his, her eyes closed.

'I must, my dear,' he said helplessly.

She leaned away and stared up at him, scared.

'Why, Harry? Where are you going?'

He shrugged.

'God knows! I shall just hump my pack and wander on till something turns up, like the soldier of fortune I am.'

'Don't go!' she said huskily.

'What else can I do, Toots? You must have seen by now that I'm no damn use to anyone,' he said, on a note of brave self-pity.

'I want you,' she said, fiercely locking her fingers in his.

He smiled down on her tenderly.

'I've done some pretty rotten things in my time, but I've never been a sponge.'

She went very white.

'Harry, I can't let you go! I love you.'

'Dear little thing!' he said.

'Oh, don't make it so hard for me,' she implored. 'Don't you understand? I'm asking you to marry me.'

★　★　★

Catherine woke early the day of the Dr. Barnardo Fete to see a curtain of fine rain swaying outside her window. This seemed like the last intolerable blow of fate. She had slept badly, pursued all night by horrible dreams from which she awoke with a thudding heart, only to slip reluctantly back into uneasy slumber. And the feeling of oppression with which she woke turned to despair at sight of the weather. While she dressed, while she combed her hair, she uttered over and over frantic, insincere little petitions: 'If it be Thy will, O Lord, if it be Thy will, let it be fine!' With the tortured superstition of the love-obsessed she ceaselessly offered up small compulsive acts of propitiation to the God of wrath.

She was so agitated that it was difficult to hide her distress from her father. As soon as she took him in his bowl of washing water, she saw that it was one of her father's bad days, one of the days when nothing she could do was right. When at last she ventured to remind him of the fete that afternoon, and to ask him whether he would like General Ridley to sit with him while she was out, he snapped back a decisive negative.

'But, Father dear, you know you don't like being left alone,' she sighed.

'The remedy for that lies with you,' he answered.

'Father dear, please be reasonable! I must go now. They're relying on me. How can I let them down at the last minute?'

'In view of the weather, it is hardly probable that there will be anyone there for you to let down. However, as I've had occasion to say to you more than once, it's entirely a matter for your own conscience to decide.'

'The general will be so disappointed. You know how much he enjoys a game of chess with you,' she coaxed.

'I should have thought the knowledge that your father was feeling too ill for visitors would have carried some weight with you.'

She said, in a voice that she could not keep from trembling slightly, 'It isn't very often that I go out anywhere.'

'Whereas your father, of course, can go wherever he likes!' He finished drying his hands and flung the towel irritably away so that it fell on the floor. 'What did you say?' he said, as she stooped to pick it up.

'I only said that you'd had your life,' she muttered.

'Ah, there speaks my Goneril! That sounds more like yourself. Reproach me for not being in my grave! Go on, stab out my eyes! There's not much else left you can take from me.'

She held up the towel between them to

hide her face as she folded it.

With a sideways glance in his shaving-mirror, the old man saw her expression. 'Oh, now, for the martyrdom of St. Catherine!' he sighed. 'Well, sooner than have you glooming at me all the afternoon with that pious, put-upon expression, you'd better go, since that seems to be your only wish, your sole consideration. Better to suffer an attack while I'm alone than have to endure that reproachful, injured look of yours.'

'No, Father, I won't leave you, if that's how you feel,' Catherine said bitterly.

★ ★ ★

By midday, the rain had ceased, leaving the sky a brilliant dishevelled blue with great glittering clouds tumbling out of sight behind roofs and trees and hills. The sun was mirrored in hundreds of glistening leaves as they tossed in the breeze. The air was fresh and rich with scents, and birds flew in and out of the branches, rocking jubilantly on their twigs and singing. The ground would still be soggy underfoot (Colonel

Fitzalan, who was lending his garden for the occasion, thought sadly of the damage to his lawns from the ladies' spiky heels) but it would clearly be fine enough to erect the stalls and marquees out of doors.

Sometimes it seemed to Naomi when Crispin was at work in her attic studio that the persistent irregular stroke of her hammer was tapping on her nerves. Today, her head ached, and the pecking noise seemed to aggravate it. But of course it would never do to ask Crispin to stop it for a while; she had been taught the heinousness of that. It was the very last issue on which she might expect consideration from Crispin.

Naomi tentatively put her head round the studio door.

She said brightly, 'Luncheon's ready when you are, darling.'

Crispin tapped on.

'I made it early,' Naomi went on, 'because of the Garden Fete this afternoon. I thought possibly you might like to go for a while.'

'I can't. I shall be working.'

Naomi's quick temper flared out in disappointment.

'Whenever there's a chance of our going out together, you're always too busy. It's funny!'

'My good Ryder, I can't stop work just because you can shut up shop.'

'Oh, of course, compared with an artist, a mere tradesman's life is incomparably luxurious and idle,' Naomi said with a sardonic smile.

* * *

'My dear, what is the matter?' Mrs. Verney said to Catherine as they met by chance in the Post Office.

'It's nothing. Truly,' Catherine muttered, turning away her head. 'It's just that Father's been a little trying this morning.'

'What a shame, you poor child!'

Beside herself, Catherine suddenly burst out:

'I never do leave him, everyone knows that. I suppose I should never have promised to help at the fete: I might have known he'd find some way to stop me.' Her voice broke. She blew her nose. 'He resents me having any pleasure.'

'What's the trouble?'

'He won't be alone. And he won't have any of his friends to sit with him. He simply wants to make it impossible for me to go. I wouldn't care for myself, except that I promised ... ' She quavered. 'I ... And I hate to let people down at the last moment.'

'But you shall go, my dear child. Why ever not? I'll keep an eye on your father. I won't sit with him, so he won't feel he has the need to entertain me, but he'll know he's not alone. No need for you to worry. It'll do him good not to get his own way for once. You run along and enjoy yourself!' the fairy godmother said gaily.

* * *

'I promised I'd look in at Chetwynd House for a minute this afternoon, if I possibly can find time. Would you like me to come back for you?' Robert said to his wife at luncheon.

His wife — leaning her head on her hand with a preoccupied expression — did not hear him, and he was obliged to repeat it.

'Heaven forbid!' she declared then, with

a wry face. 'Whatever for?'

'I thought it might take you out of yourself. You stick at home too much, brooding; it's not good for you.'

'I'm quite staggered by this sudden consideration. I hope it isn't the sign of an uneasy conscience,' said his wife.

'It's rather that I feel one ought to do one's bit to make these affairs a success.'

'Well, if they're raffling a bottle of whisky, I'm willing to contribute half-a-crown in raffle tickets for it. You can lay it out for me,' she said, dropping her crumpled napkin onto her plate as she rose from the table.

★   ★   ★

Light breezes shook down pendants of silver drops from the trees overhead ... Fat old village women bumbled along like tops on their painful feet ... In summer dresses bright as flowers, slender girls with clouds of hair raced about in the pride of their youth ... Squeals and laughter rose on the air ...

Janet Scott was shouting:

'Walk up! Walk up! Three tries for

sixpence, and a loverly cokernut for the winner!'

As Edward Golding walked past, she broke off to call to him:

'Ned, be a saint and bring me a lemonade or a cup of tea or something. I'm so hoarse I can hardly croak.'

He raised a finger in acknowledgment. But outside the marquee he collared one of his boys and told him to take a glass of squash to Miss Scott.

* * *

And, after all, Crispin did not work that afternoon. Once the front door had slammed behind Naomi, Crispin cast down her tools to watch, with a sulky eye, from the window as she trotted down the street in her best navy print. Crispin lit a cigar and paced up and down the studio, eyeing the block of stone with a hideous frown. Then, with an exclamation, she seized a jacket and ran out of the house in the opposite direction from Naomi.

Editha was in her garden at the back of the old stone house, standing motionless among the lavender bushes with a hand to her brow. She turned with a frown of annoyance as Crispin exclaimed behind her:

'Lady thinking her lavender thoughts!'

Editha uttered a short laugh.

'Have you ever wanted to kill anyone? That was the lavender thought occupying my mind at that moment.'

'How delightfully human of you, my dear!' Crispin cried. 'Was I to be the victim? What a voluptuous death, to be killed by that exquisite hand.'

Editha looked at her contemptuously.

'Why on earth should I want to kill you?' she said in a tone that clearly placed Crispin's unimportance to her.

'Robert, then?' Crispin said hopefully.

Editha said, 'What can make you suppose that I would want to kill my husband?'

'Darling, who else could you want to kill? You surely wouldn't bother to murder even in your thoughts that silly young woman.'

'What young woman?'

'Don't be stuffy, darling; not with me. You're surely not going to pretend that no one has yet dared to tell you about her? You're not going to pretend that you mind about that dull little man's dull little *affaire*?'

With a curious expression on her face, Editha broke off a sprig of lavender and held it to her nose.

★　★　★

Catherine watched Dr. Mansbridge in his dark lounge suit threading his way through the crowd, pausing to speak to this one and that with his genial smile. A pulse began beating heavily in her throat, and she bent her head as if unaware of his approach.

'Please, miss, I've come for me penn'orth of sweeties,' he said comically, touching his hat.

'Oh, Doctor! I didn't see you,' she stammered, the blood quickening in her cheeks.

'I know. You were so busy calculating your profits that I almost crept away without disturbing you,' he said with a friendly laugh. 'Now then, what have you got?'

'There's fudge,' she said, 'and caramels, or peppermint creams.'

'What do you recommend?'

'I don't know,' she murmured stupidly, staring at him with large eyes.

'Well, I'll take a bag of fudge, I think.'

She stooped and handed him one from the back of the counter.

'Oh, can't I have one of these pretty ones?'

She began to stammer again:

'They're really just for display. Besides, they'd be a bit sticky, I'm afraid, from lying in the sun all this while. I could take one of the ribbons off, if you liked, to fasten yours.'

He laughed.

'No, no, it doesn't matter.' He waited, looking at her with an amused expression. 'Well,' he said at last, 'aren't you going to ask me for my money?'

'Oh, I forgot,' she said with a nervous laugh. 'That will be three shillings.' As he turned over the coins in his palm, she said, 'May I wish you a very happy holiday, in case I don't see you again before you go?' She fumbled for something to say that would keep him a moment longer. 'Will you send me a postcard from Cornwall?' At his involuntary look of surprise, she felt herself blush. 'I collect them, I mean,' she stammered.

'I must try and remember that,' he said, with good-natured courtesy so that she should not guess he was embarrassed by her lapse of taste. He raised his hat again, and was gone.

It was over.

She watched him blankly as he moved through the crowd, pausing to laugh and talk, tossing pennies into a bucket, throwing darts at a board, drifting away out of her sight.

★　★　★

'I wasn't being malicious,' Crispin insisted. 'I naturally supposed you knew about it, my dear. Everyone else does. I never dreamed you'd mind.'

'I don't. I know Robert, you see.'

'Then why abuse me so for telling you?'

'Perhaps to punish you for impertinence,' Editha said with a crooked smile. 'I happen not to care for gossip. It's not only ugly in itself, it usually has an ugly purpose behind it,' she enunciated the last phrase slowly, so that Crispin could not fail to understand. She looked at her sardonically from under drooping lids. "The dog, to gain some private end, went mad and bit the man',' she remarked drily.

Crispin flushed.

'My only ulterior motive is to want to see you happy — if you consider that an ugly purpose ... '

'And you expect to achieve that by telling me that my husband is unfaithful to me?' said Editha in the same dry tone.

'I hate to see you wasting your life on someone so utterly unworthy of you, if you must know.'

'You think I should leave him? And go away with you, no doubt?'

'I ask nothing better,' said Crispin lightly.

'Where, for instance?'

'Anywhere you pleased. You have only to say. Have you ever been to Spain? I'd love to take you to Madrid, to the Prado to see the El Grecos. Did I ever tell you that you look like an El Greco?'

'Frequently. Well, Spain would do. When do we start?'

'As soon as you like,' said Crispin, lighting a cigarette.

'Next week, then. Robert goes off for a fortnight's fishing then in Cornwall, and afterwards we're to go to Portugal. It should be quite easy for me to go from Spain to meet him there.'

Crispin stared.

'You're not serious?'

'Why not? You're always asking me to run away with you. Well, I've agreed.' She burst into laughter. 'Oh, my dear Leslie, if you could only see your face! The consternation!'

Crispin swung down from the low wall where she was perched.

'It's not consternation, it's incredulity!'

'But why should you be so astonished? You've persuaded me. You've overcome my scruples at last,' said Editha, breaking into mirth again.

Crispin frowned. 'You're in a frightfully jokey mood all of a sudden. Do you really want to come away with me?'

'Why shouldn't I have a little fun before I die? I can hardly think it would be more tedious than watching Robert fish all day.'

'Won't Robert object?'

'Why on earth should he?' said Editha with a cold stare.

Crispin caught her hands.

'You extraordinary person,' she muttered. 'If you're playing with me … '

★ ★ ★

Naomi Ryder was enjoying herself. She had won a pullet in a raffle, and a dumpy brown teapot — oddly like herself — at hoopla, and now she was absorbed in rolling pennies down a slide. She bought some more change from Miss Lucas, and was just laughing at some remark of hers when her eyes, wandering idly over the sunny scene, caught sight of Crispin — with 'that woman' — winding through the people at the entrance. At once, all her pleasure vanished, and a sullen look settled over her pretty features; she rapidly rolled the coins down the slide one after the other and turned away without waiting to see where they fell.

If it could be any consolation to Naomi, Mrs. Mansbridge was having a bad moment too. Almost the first person she saw as she entered the garden was Harry with little Mrs. Petrie bouncing along on his arm.

'Do you know that man, darling?' Crispin said, following her gaze.

'Why should I?' Editha said frigidly.

'Only because I saw you staring at them. There's a fine story going the rounds about them. But I forgot,' said Crispin, with a teasing glance, 'you're not interested in gossip.'

'That depends what it is. What do they say?'

'Well, my dear, only — if you can imagine it! — that the two of them run a *maison de rendezvous*!'

Editha said, 'There's Miss Ryder. Don't you want to go and speak to her?'

'No, thank you, darling, I've spoken to her already today.'

All Crispin's exhibitionism, manifested in her eccentric clothes and habits, now came to the fore. She entered into the spirit of the thing with such zest that she had a little crowd following her from sideshow to sideshow. She was laughing loudly and cracking jokes with the bystanders in aristocratic bonhomie. It was also an outlet for the elation which filled her. At any other time, such exuberance would have displeased Editha, but now she hardly noticed it, occupied as she was in following Harry's progress out of the corner of her eye. Seeing him enter the marquee alone,

Editha slipped away and drifted after him into the tent. She chose her moment; and, as she passed him casually, said in a sharp, commanding undertone: 'I must speak to you. Come round tomorrow morning after surgery.'

'Gracious lady!' Harry murmured with a cool, small bow.

★ ★ ★

Thankfully Janet handed over to Mr. Lawrence and wandered away to take a little amusement herself. It was amazing how quickly the pennies and sixpences disappeared at the sideshows; in a short while she had spent all the money she had with her. She stood in a crowd watching people throw tennis balls into a pail. Edward Golding was nearby. She moved through the group towards him. She caught his sleeve, ' "Bozzy, lend me sixpence; not to be repaid",' she quoted.

A shade of annoyance appeared to cloud for a moment his face but he made no comment, merely pulling out a handful of silver and offering it to her on his palm. She picked out some coins, looking up at him with her mischievous smile. 'How have you managed to hang on to all this money, you miser?'

'I've been lucky,' he said lightly.

'Well, if you bring me luck with this lot, I'll stand you a beer afterwards.' Nonchalantly she tucked a drooping handkerchief back into his breast pocket, and he quickly brushed her hand away as if it had been an unwelcome insect. With a hasty glance behind him, he muttered, 'Don't do that!'

'Sorry,' Janet said with a look of astonishment. 'Sorry, I'm sure.'

He walked away without answering. She stared after him in bewilderment: it was so totally unlike Ned to snarl at a person over nothing. She bit her lip and frowned. In some way she must have offended him. How silly, she thought; between *us*! Impetuously, she ran after him and caught up with him outside the refreshment tent, among the trampled grass, the sweet papers and the cigarette ends. The afternoon was petering out in squalor and exhaustion.

She said gently, 'Ned! Is anything the matter?'

Again she noticed the quick, hunted look he cast behind him. He ran his tongue between his lips.

'Look, Janet,' he said earnestly, 'don't follow me about, there's a good girl.'

'Follow you about?' she echoed. 'I'm not following you, my dear man. Whatever gave you that idea? I simply wanted to know what was wrong, that's all.'

'Nothing, nothing,' he said hastily. 'But do just ... Honestly, I don't know how to put this without sounding offensive ... but we simply cannot ... ' He hesitated.

'Oh, cough it up, Ned, whatever it is!'

'Well. To put it quite bluntly, I want you to keep away from me.'

'Keep away from you! Why? Are you contagious?'

'It's no joking matter, Janet. Just do as I ask, there's a good lass. Don't ask questions.'

'I don't understand. Is it some kind of game?'

'Far from it, I'm afraid.'

'Tell me one thing, then. Is it anything to do with me? Have I annoyed you in some way?'

'No. No, of course not,' he said quickly.

'Well, do for goodness' sake stop all this 'Hist, we are observed!' stuff, and tell me what it's all about.'

He hesitated, pursing his lips into a sort of grimace. Then he said, 'It's that damned Mrs. Doctor. She told Betsy about us.'

'The old bitch!' Janet said indignantly. 'How did she know, anyway?'

Edward Golding shrugged.

'Oh, it's evidently a matter for common gossip; it appears the entire village knows about it.'

Janet said, 'She can't possibly have *known*. She must have made it up to be spiteful; it's exactly the malevolent kind of story she does invent.'

'That's hardly the point,' he said wearily.

Janet said quickly, 'You didn't let Bets think it was true!'

'Why not?'

'Oh, you fool!' she cried. 'You damned silly fool, don't you know better than to admit a thing like that?'

'What does it matter? I told Bets it was all over ages ago.'

Janet turned away her face. There was a

look about her mouth as if she had bitten into something unexpectedly sour.

'Of course,' he said quickly, 'Betsy's too sensible to mind about what happened before we were married. But I don't want her to imagine — '

'No, of course not,' she agreed. 'And anyway, there won't be anything for her *to* imagine, will there?'

'No,' he too-readily answered. 'But you can see it isn't fair to her to let people gossip about us.'

'No, of course not,' she repeated. 'It's all right, Ned. Don't worry. I'll keep my paws off. It's just that I'm a demonstrative sort of person, you know; it doesn't really mean a thing.'

'I know, old girl. But I can hardly expect Betsy to understand that, and I'm afraid she does rather resent it when she sees us together. She's awfully young, you know.'

'Poor old Bets, it's a damned shame! Someone ought to strangle that mischief-making cow,' she observed.

'I couldn't agree with you more,' Edward Golding said heartily.

5

In a Small Beech Copse

Once again the sky was overcast, threatening rain. There was a chill in the air and the trees shuddered faintly in their thin green cloaks.

Crispin came down to the kitchen with a sullen expression, her paisley dressing-gown knotted tightly about her waist, yawning and rubbing her short gilt hair till it stood on end. Naomi, sipping a cup of tea by the stove, pointedly ignored her friend's entrance.

'What's happened to breakfast this morning?' Crispin inquired with a peevish glance at the unlaid table.

Naomi remained mute.

'Oh, it's a strike, is it?' Crispin said with a laugh. 'How childish you can be, Ryder.' She gave an enormous yawn and sauntered across to the window. 'Another bloody day,' she commented, staring out. 'How this place gets on my nerves! How deathly sick I am of it all!'

Naomi, though she had sworn herself to silence, could not forbear saying:

'What you really mean is that you're sick of me, don't you?'

Somewhat to her surprise Crispin turned on her a charming smile.

'Frankly, my dear, we have rather been getting on each other's nerves lately,' she said magnanimously. 'I dare say it's been my fault. I think I need a change. I've been working too hard lately and I've gone stale. I think it would do me good to get away for a bit, right away from everything.'

'Yes?' said Naomi on an indifferent note. She could not help a wry smile twisting her lips at this typical Crispinism. '*I* am the one who works like a slave,' she thought, 'but *she* is the one who needs a holiday, though she has been away twice this year already.' Of course she realized that Crispin was using this as an excuse, perhaps to break with her for ever. A sudden disagreeable notion presented itself to her, and she found a bitter pleasure in saying:

'You'll go to Cornwall, I suppose.'

'To Cornwall?' said Crispin with an innocent blue stare. 'Why on earth Cornwall?'

'I understood that was where the Mansbridges are going this year.'

'Really?' said Crispin, lighting a cigarette. 'I wouldn't know. I shall be going to Spain, if you're interested.'

Once again, Naomi betrayed the hopeless vulgarity of her plebian mind by jeering, 'Don't tell me you've quarrelled with the divine Editha! I thought she could never do anything wrong in your eyes. Or have I got hold of the wrong end of the stick? Perhaps you've managed to persuade her to go with you at last!' She laughed. Her intention was only to be mildly malicious, but she chanced to glance at Crispin from the corner of her eye as she spoke, and was stabbed by the instant conviction that she had accidentally hit on the truth. *They were going away together.* For a moment, Naomi's mind went quite blank, and she was almost as surprised as Crispin to see her cup sail through the air and strike the window frame beside Crispin's head.

Crispin was genuinely flabbergasted at this — as it seemed — unprovoked assault.

But she only said quite patiently, tapping the ash from her cigarette onto the clean-washed tiles, 'What on earth is the matter with you this morning, Ryder?'

'God, how I despise you!' Naomi cried. 'Did you imagine I wouldn't guess you were going off with *her*?' She was shaking with nervous rage.

Crispin eyed her coldly.

'Well, what of it?' she said at last.

'So you don't deny it?'

'Why should I?'

'All right,' Naomi said in a trembling voice. 'All right! But understand one thing. You needn't think you can come back here afterwards. I'm finished with you. Do you hear? I'm finished. I've had as much as I can stand.'

'Why, do you know? So have I,' said Crispin pleasantly; and, tossing her cigarette out of the window, she strolled from the room.

'You'll find two can play at this game!' Naomi shouted after her, beside herself with fury. But there was no reply. She subsided weakly on to a chair and leaned on the table. For a long time she sat there like a stone, staring at the broken fragments on the floor in their little pool of tea-leaves ...

The rain drummed suddenly down like the beginning of an ominous overture.

★   ★   ★

As soon as surgery was over and the doctor had gone out, Mrs. Mansbridge sent Norah into the village on errands it would take her at least an hour to execute. She wished to be alone when Harry came. She stationed herself to watch for him.

He came at last, shaking the rain from his clothes like a dog. 'Madam wished to see me?' he said in his insolent manner.

Mrs. Mansbridge said, 'Come inside. And shut the door.'

★   ★   ★

Mrs. Petrie glanced up and saw Harry standing in the doorway, biting his thumb with a preoccupied expression.

'Hullo, darling. Lunch is nearly ready,' she said.

'I've got to go away,' he said.

She said gaily, 'Well, not before you've had lunch, I hope. I'll go and lay the table now.'

'I'd better pack,' he said, turning to the staircase door.

'Pack?' she echoed in consternation. 'You're not going away?'

'I've just told you I am.'

'But, darling, I thought you meant ... Where are you going, then?'

'Oh, something rather unforeseen has turned up,' he said casually. 'Just one of those things.

'It's not bad news, is it, darling?' she said anxiously.

'Good Lord, no,' he said brightly. 'Don't panic, Toots. I'll be back.'

At once she abandoned the pan she was stirring over the flame and ran to him, her face puckered with fear.

'Harry,' she said, 'you're not leaving me? You wouldn't do that — not now. Swear, Harry!'

'Don't be silly, Toots,' he said, and gave her an affectionate pinch.

⋆   ⋆   ⋆

It was nearly half-past one when Dr. Mansbridge returned. Miss Ryder was leaving the house as he entered the gate. She looked so unlike her cheerful ruddy self that for a split-second he didn't know her. She passed him with a blank stare, no recognition in her eyes. He raised his brows in faint perplexity, and then with a shrug entered the house.

Only one place was laid in the dining-room, and when Norah came in, Dr. Mansbridge said, 'Is Mrs. Mansbridge out to lunch?'

'No, sir.'

'Oh, then she's already had it, has she?' he said, seating himself.

The maid hesitated. 'Well, no, sir, not exactly.'

'What do you mean?'

'Madam did tell me not to mention it to you, she didn't want you to be bothered, but she wouldn't take any lunch. She went up to her room and said she wanted to be left alone.'

Dr. Mansbridge pushed back his chair.

'I'd better go and see,' he muttered. 'Take the food back and keep it warm, Norah.'

He ran upstairs.

'Editha?' he called, rattling the handle. There was no answer. He rapped and called again.

'What is it?' she cried from within.

'Open the door, Editha. I want to come in.'

'I left a message that I didn't want to be disturbed. I've got a headache. Didn't Norah tell you?'

'Please let me in, dear. I want to speak to you.' He could hear her grousing to herself as she approached and unlocked the door. They stood confronting each other suspiciously.

'Can't I have even half an hour to myself?' she complained.

'I only came to see what's the matter, why you didn't want any lunch?'

'I told you, I've got a headache.'

But he could smell the whisky on her breath and his mouth tightened with impatience.

He said roughly, 'Headache, my foot!' and pushed past her into the room. He saw almost at once the bottle and glass on the desk where she had been writing when he interrupted her. He said angrily, 'Really, Editha, you're the most troublesome and uncooperative of all my patients. How many whiskies have you had this morning?'

'Oh, don't be such a bloody bore, Robert,' she said with an angry laugh. 'You talk as if I was a confirmed drunkard. If you only knew how ridiculous you sound when you're being pompous!'

He said, with an effort at patience, 'My dear good woman, what does it matter to me if you drink? I'm simply tired of telling you the harm you are doing yourself by drinking in your condition. Do you want to kill yourself?'

'It would suit you nicely if I did, no doubt,' she countered.

'That would hardly seem to be my aim,' he murmured as he stooped to pick up a crumpled sheet of writing-paper off the floor. He smoothed it absently and, without intending to, saw Editha's familiar scribble — *My dear Leslie, you say you would do anything for me* — before he screwed it up again and tossed it into the waste-paper basket.

His wife was watching him through

narrowed eyes. The whisky she had taken, on top of the strain of her interview with Harry, unleashed her bitter spleen.

'Oh, no, it would never do to let it be seen that you want me out of the way. You must at all costs keep up appearances.'

He said calmly, 'Don't be so silly, dear.'

'I suppose if I were dead you'd marry the girl?'

He turned on her a wide uncomprehending stare.

'I'm afraid I haven't the least idea what you're talking about.'

His air of innocence was like paraffin to the spark of her anger. She flared out:

'Oh, for God's sake! If you imagine that I don't know, that I haven't heard — in a village like this — all the squalid details, you must be uncommonly stupid. I could even name the hotel you go to in Cambury, if you want proof.'

'Can I possibly prevail on you to give me some idea what this is all about?'

She folded her arms across her bosom, gripping her upper arms tightly, and forced herself to speak in a level tone to match his own.

'Must you really be quite so naive, Robert? I'm not trying to trap you, believe me. And if your intention is to spare my feelings, you needn't bother. I'm not jealous.'

'You have no cause to be.'

'Your line is, I suppose,' she said sardonically (but she was shaking with rage), 'that your love for me is unimpaired and that the little drab means nothing to you.'

'This is a strange accusation to level at me. You sound to me quite out of your mind, my dear Editha. Or are you ill?' He moved towards her to lay a hand on her brow, but she slapped it away sharply, crying: 'Don't touch me! Don't dare!'

He drew back and stared at her critically.

'May one at least ask who this 'little drab', as you call it, is supposed to be?'

Editha uttered a dry laugh.

'You would prefer me to call her by some more highfalutin name, no doubt: your mistress, your lady-love,' she suggested.

He said coolly, 'I have no mistress. As you must know perfectly well. This is one of your more fantastic delusions.'

'And is everyone else in the village

suffering from the same delusion? Are you a complete and utter fool,' she raged, 'or merely a hypocrite? Is it her name you are trying to protect or your own? I must say,' she went wildly wandering on, 'that with your almost neurotic concern about the proprieties, I do wonder at your conducting such a sordid little *affaire* on your own doorstep. Or were you so bemused with lust that you were lost to all sense of danger?' Her burning eyes devoured him, and then suddenly she burst out laughing, right in his frowning face. He stared at her in amazement. Her laughter rose: shrill, convulsive, uncontrollable. 'I've only just seen ... ' She tried to explain through her mirth. 'God, how dense of me ... Now I know why you're looking so ... so po-faced and innocent ... it's the thought of your precious career ... I might have known, that's all you care about ... And you're scared to death I'll divorce you and name her as co-respondent ... and that would mean the B.M.A. down on you like a load of bricks ... and the noble (oh, my God!) self-sacrificing doctor s-s-struck off the register ... for unprofessional conduct ... ' She was gasping with the exhaustion of hysteria, black tears running off her eyelashes and down her cheeks.

He said sharply: 'Stop that! Stop laughing like that!'

'Oh, God, your face ... ' she cried, putting a handkerchief to her wet eyes. 'You don't see the joke ... poor Robert ... I so nearly made a damned fool of myself. You'd have had all the cards ... if you only knew ... I'd sooner kill myself than let you — '

Norah, listening eagerly on the stairs, heard a small, crisp explosion, like a paper bag bursting, and caught her breath with excitement.

Mrs. Mansbridge cried out:

'You loathsome brute! You struck me!'

The doctor said coldly:

'You're hysterical!'

'I'm not in the least hysterical, you humourless fool. Will you please stop looking at me like that!' she screamed, stamping her foot.

'You'd better lie down,' he replied in a maddeningly calm, even voice. 'I'll get you a draught.'

'You smug, unmitigated cad!' she yelled after him as he left the room. 'You'll not get away with it, I promise you. You'll not get away with it!'

Norah scuffled wildly down the stairs, her heart beating with excitement. This was the first real row she'd ever had the good fortune to catch them at.

When Dr. Mansbridge got back with the draught, Editha's rage had dissolved into tears of self-pity. He sat down on the bed beside her, put an arm round her shoulders and persuaded her to drink the sedative. He neither reproached her for the scene nor tried further to convince her that she was under an illusion; he simply made her comfortable on the bed and left her.

Norah was arranging her headscarf in front of the cracked mirror on the wall when the doctor entered the kitchen and said:

'Your mistress would like a cup of tea; she's not feeling very well.'

'You're telling me!' Norah said to herself, but she merely showed him a sulky face and said, 'I'm just off, sir. I want to catch the bus.'

'I didn't know it was your day off.'

'Madam said I could have this afternoon

because I gave up my day to oblige her.'

'All right,' he said. 'Cut along, then. I'll do it myself.'

'Your dinner's in the oven, keeping warm,' she informed him kindly as she swung out of the door.

It was half-past two when at last Dr. Mansbridge came to his meal. The food was dry and unattractive, and he demolished it quickly, without relish, a book propped up before him. When he had stacked the dishes tidily in the sink, he went to his surgery. There was a great deal of paperwork to be got through, and he tackled it in the same neat and methodical way he went at any tedious task.

It was nearly five when at last he stretched wearily back in his chair and flexed his stiff fingers. Before he started on his evening round, he went upstairs to see if Editha wanted anything.

She was asleep: her spectacles on her nose and the *Life of Lady Hamilton,* fallen from her grasp, lying open on the coverlet beside the little bag of sweets. Gently, he removed the spectacles and folded them into their case, then tucked the coverlet more comfortably about the sleeping woman's shoulders, and closed the door quietly behind him.

Dr. Mansbridge's evening round took a considerable time: there were so many patients to be visited in outlying hamlets, and a second visit back to the nursing-home where there was a woman in labour. The child was delivered safely soon after eight-thirty, and by then the doctor was weary and would have been glad to go home. But he was not allowed to escape the little ceremony with the matron. She nabbed him just as he had finished cleaning himself, and swept him off to her sitting-room for a nice chat. As usual, there was a tray of sandwiches and tea unobtrusively waiting for him. That was Matron's little plot, a small gratification of her secret weakness, for she nourished a soft, an almost mushy, spot for him in her starched bosom. She could see as well as anybody else that his wife did not look after him properly, it was shameful, but at least she could see to it that he had something to eat when he came under her roof. She poured him a third cup of mahogany tea: he had eaten the sandwiches without noticing.

It was soon after nine when he left the nursing-home. The sky had cleared after the rain and the evening was warm and sunny. Birds wheeled in droves across the clear gold sky, crying as they flew. The rhythmic beat and high voices calling came from the tennis courts beyond the river, and the agreeable sounds of children shouting at play, rose on the air. In the leaf-shadowed lanes, girls in bright summer frocks loitered, exchanging pert cries with the youths shooting heroically among them on their bicycles. It was an evening that called for enjoyment.

Dr. Mansbridge hesitated with a hand on the door of his car. The thought of returning home filled him with a weary distaste. His lungs seemed full of stale air, his mind of stale thoughts. He got into the car, and with sudden decision, let in the clutch.

★　★　★

The placid beauty of the evening, the glorious light slanting low across the village, did nothing to calm Catherine or assuage her anguish of mind. The golden hills shimmered to her tear-filled eyes. She was stifled by a queer blend of excitement and dread. All day an unbearable restlessness had grown upon her, the walls seeming to press in on her like her suffocating thoughts. Her fingers plucked at the honeysuckle round her bedroom window and tore the fragrant blossoms to shreds. She longed to run somewhere, to tell someone. But there was nowhere to run, and the secret must be borne in silence — for ever. 'God,' she prayed, biting her knuckles. 'Oh, God, help me!' And then she saw the doctor's car, and watched it drive out of the village along the dusty white lane for a quarter of a mile and draw to a halt. The doctor got out and disappeared among the trees. He was alone. God, she thought, had heard her cry. He was offering her a chance, before it was too late ...

★   ★   ★

Mrs. Verney rose from her knees in the front garden and pulled off her leather gloves to light a fresh cigarette. As she did so, she saw Catherine come out of the gate opposite and hurry down the lane in the opposite direction

148

from the village. That was the way people went for country walks, and surely Catherine wouldn't be doing that. You'd have thought from her haste that she was going to an assignation. A strange girl, mused Mrs. Verney, dropping onto her knees again.

⋆　⋆　⋆

Some way beyond the village was a small beech copse, a thing of beauty at this time of year with the light filtering down through layer after layer of brilliant green leaves on to its innumerable narrow mossy paths. A pleasant place to walk, and Dr. Mansbridge had not been there for years until this evening.

Good-natured though he was, he had had such a day of it that he was faintly irritated to run into anyone he knew and have his pleasant solitude disturbed.

He greeted her politely because it was too late to pretend he had not seen her.

'I had no idea this was a haunt of yours,' he said pleasantly. 'Lovely evening, isn't it?' He raised his hat and would have walked on, but she suddenly broke from her rigid pose and plunged forward, catching at his sleeve like a drowning person. Yes, in that greenish underwater light with her white staring face, she did look as if she was drowning.

'Doctor, I must speak to you!' She gulped out the words.

'Why, certainly, Miss Duncton. Nothing wrong, I hope?' But he really felt he could bear no more just then of human problems and pains. For once he determined to keep it at bay — whatever it was — if he could.

She stumbled along at his side. The path was so narrow there was scarcely room for two to walk abreast, and she wondered that he did not hear the thudding of her heart.

'Are you playing truant too?' he said. 'I suppose I ought really to be at home cutting the grass, but it seemed too fine an evening to waste. It does us all good to break away sometimes.'

At this, a raucous laugh echoed through the trees. 'There's the green woodpecker.' He smiled.

With an enormous effort, she broke in:

'Dr. Mansbridge, there's something I must tell you ... I can't go on like this ... '

Her chest heaved with the sobs she strove to stifle.

Here it came after all, he thought.

'Steady, now,' he said gently, 'take it easy.'

To her shame, the tears burst from her helplessly at his kind tone.

'I'm sorry,' she sobbed, 'I'm sorry.'

'Come, now,' he said, 'you're spoiling a pleasant evening. Dry your eyes and forget your troubles. They're never as important as they seem to us at the time. When things become difficult, we tend to lose our sense of proportion.'

'You don't understand,' she said hoarsely.

'I understand enough to know you're not happy. Don't try to explain, it only makes it more painful for you, believe me. It won't always be like this, you know. One day you'll be free,' he said with brisk confidence, lifting away the leafy branches that barred the path.

'Free?' She tasted the word incredulously. 'Do you dream of freedom too?'

'I'm afraid I'm too prosaic for such romantic fancies.' He laughed.

'You said once that you longed to be free,' she reminded him.

'I did,' he said, puzzled.

He couldn't have forgotten, she thought; he *couldn't*. She turned back to the problem of herself.

She said, on a note of ludicrous despair: 'I'm twenty-seven.'

'One foot in the grave,' he said, laughing.

There was something rather moving, rather beautiful, in the way her eyes, still abrim with tears, flashed at him.

'Do you think it's funny to see one's life wasting away, year after year, in futile sacrifice? Haven't I the right to happiness, like anyone else?'

'Of course.'

She flushed.

'I know it's wicked of me, but when I think that Father may live another twenty years, I hate him. What use will my life be to me then? It will all have been for nothing.'

Dr. Mansbridge said, 'You know, I have always found it a remarkably good plan not to look too far ahead. We can none of us know what the future will bring — which may be just as well,' he added. 'To look ahead for twenty years only makes the present seem more intolerable. In difficult situations it is better to live a day at a time. Indeed, sometimes it is the only way to get through a bad patch,' he sighed.

'I think it is only when one is unhappy in the present that one does look into the future,' Catherine said in a low voice. 'It is a sort of escape into a prospect of happiness.'

'Oh, things are never so bad that they mightn't be worse,' Dr. Mansbridge declared cheerfully. 'You should take up some hobby, you know. You'd be surprised what a difference it would make to your outlook to have some outside interest.'

The sun drifting down the sky cast shafts of ruddy light through the interstices of the leaves. The wood was full of liquid trills and calls as the birds scattered to their nests. Catherine uttered a cry and clapped a hand to her face. She had let go of a branch too soon, and it had swung back and caught her in the eye. She stood there, stunned with the shock of the pain.

'What's the matter?' said Dr. Mansbridge, turning back. 'Let me see.'

She removed her hand for a moment,

and then hurriedly clapped it back. He pulled away her fingers and saw a red mark like a lash on her cheek. She blinked up at him, her eye watering furiously in the light. She looked away, screwing up her face.

'Keep still,' he commanded, holding her chin steady with one hand and gently prying the lids apart with the other while he peered at the pupil. His face was so close that she could see the tender liquid tea-colour of his eyes. He was close ... It made her dizzy ...

With an abruptness that took them both by surprise, she twisted round and pressed her mouth passionately into the palm of his hand.

As though the kiss had burned it, he snatched his hand away.

They stared at one another. She put a clenched fist against her mouth with a faint moan.

'I didn't mean ... ' she said. 'I don't know what happened ... I couldn't help myself ... I lost my head ... It was dreadful ... I don't know what you must think of me ... You've been so kind, and this evening, suddenly I felt — '

He tried to pass it off with awkward good humour, but the girl said with the fierceness of desperation:

'I'm so terribly in love with you!'

He stared incredulously.

'My dear young lady!' he protested.

She said hoarsely, 'I've been in love with you for years. I thought you had guessed.'

'No.'

'I couldn't stand it any longer. I tried ... ' She put her face into her hands. 'I suppose you're horrified. I suppose it was dreadful of me to tell you.'

'I'm not in the least horrified. But I am sorry. Though it's a thing that happens to most of us at one time or another in our lives.'

She took away her hands and shot him a quick glance, pathetic in its flinching eagerness.

'You're really not angry? I was so afraid you'd be — disgusted,' she whispered, her voice falling almost inaudibly on the last word.

'Now, why should it disgust me? You wouldn't expect me to evince disgust if you came to me and said you were starving. You've been starved emotionally, and in this way you try to compensate for your hunger. There's absolutely no need to feel ashamed of anything so natural. At your age, falling in love, as they call it, is a normal physiological occurrence. It's Nature's way of continuing the race, so She implants in you this instinct to find a mate and bear children.' He smiled at her. 'Unfortunately, Dame Nature isn't very discriminating. She's so eager to get to work on us that it makes her clumsy, with the result that we don't always fall in love with a suitable person; and then, for a time, I'm afraid, we suffer. But it passes, you know,' he said. 'You'll fall in love again. You may fall in love many times before you find the person you want to marry.'

'Oh, no! No! You don't understand. It's not like that a bit. I shall *never* love anyone else,' she cried passionately.

He could not help smiling.

'You think I'm being stupid and insensitive, I know. When we are in love we always think it is going to last for ever. Because the emotion is so intense we imagine it must be eternal. But the real tragedy of love, believe

156

me, is that it doesn't last,' he said with a wry smile.

Catherine's eyes went quickly over his face. He no longer loved his wife: he was telling her so. She had always been certain of it in her deepest heart, but that he should confide it to her just now sent a ray of joy quivering through her and the unbearable tension of guilt relaxed.

'I'll wager,' he was saying cheerfully, 'that a year from now you'll wonder how you could ever have fancied yourself in love with such a dull old fogey as me.'

She shook her head. He didn't understand, but it no longer mattered.

'Look!' he said and pointed to the yellow moon riding above the treetops.

'Oh, my goodness!' she exclaimed, as frightened as a truant child to realize how late it must be. 'I must go back at once. Father will be furious, he doesn't know I'm out. I left him listening to Strindberg on the Third Programme.' She sighed. 'I wish they did his plays more often; there's so little he really enjoys.'

For some reason Dr. Mansbridge seemed to find this amusing, but she did not mind him laughing at her.

'What funny creatures we humans are! It doesn't do to take ourselves too seriously.'

As they came out of the copse, the hills were already black against the darkening sky.

'I must go,' she said again, and held out her hand shyly.

'I'll run you back in the car.'

He dropped her at the top of her lane and drove home, his shameful platitudes still ringing in his ears. Once he took his hand off the wheel and turned it palm upwards, as though he could yet feel the kiss scalding it. 'A man of my age!' he thought.

When he entered his house, the maid was standing in the hall in her outdoor clothes. She looked frightened.

He said sharply, 'What's the matter, Norah?'

'Oh, sir!' she burst out in a catlike wail. At the same moment, a voice cut in from above:

'Mansbridge! My dear fellow, where have you been?' Dr. Horace ran downstairs with a grave face. 'We've been trying everywhere to get hold of you for the last two hours.'

'What's the matter?' Dr. Mansbridge said, not moving.

'I'm afraid this will come as a great shock to you. Mrs. Mansbridge is dead.'

The maid's loud sobs confused him; he could not think with all that racket going on.

'For goodness' sake, be quiet, Norah,' he said sharply. 'What happened, Horace?' he said, turning to the doctor.

'Believe me, we did all we could. But we were too late to save her.'

Oh, damn the old fool! Why couldn't he utter a plain statement of fact? Dr. Mansbridge steadied himself with a hand on the banisters and looked up the tall staircase as if it was the face of a mountain he had to climb.

'I shouldn't go up just yet,' said old Dr. Horace, with a restraining hand on his arm, 'the police are there.'

* * *

The questions seemed to go on for hours. 'When did you last see your wife ... ? You noticed nothing unusual about her, she

159

did not seem in any way unlike herself … ? You say she was lying down asleep when you left the house. Was that because she was unwell … ? Well, did she normally lie down in the afternoon … ? But weren't you surprised … ? Was she in the habit of taking drugs … ? Had she access to any narcotics … ? Doubtless it has slipped your mind, but I should tell you that a box of sodium amylobarbitone capsules was found in your bathroom cupboard.'

'Oh, those,' Dr. Mansbridge said, passing a hand across his brow. 'I'd forgotten. They were some I put up for myself earlier in the year. I was sleeping badly. My wife never took anything like that. I doubt if she knew they were there.'

'Can you remember how many were left in the box?'

'I'm afraid not.' He tried to think. 'I wouldn't have taken more than two or three myself.'

'And how many would you have made up altogether?'

He said vaguely, 'A dozen, perhaps.'

'There are three left.'

'It might have been only half a dozen,' he

said, rubbing his forehead.

'We needn't pursue that at present. It can, no doubt, be verified later if necessary,' said the superintendent. 'Now, the maid said you had told her she could take the afternoon off. Is that correct?'

'Why, yes. She told me that my wife had already arranged it with her, and there was no reason why she should not go.'

'It did not seem to you necessary for anyone to remain in the house with your wife?'

'Not in the least. She wasn't ill. Besides, I was here myself for the greater part of the afternoon.'

'At what time did you leave?'

'About five. I came up before I left to see if she wanted anything, but she was asleep. I didn't disturb her — she looked very comfortable — ' He broke off and, after a moment, added, 'She'd been reading her book and eating the fudge I'd brought her. How could I have supposed anything was wrong? I can't believe it was. Whatever happened must have happened later.'

'Fudge, did you say, sir?' interrupted the superintendent. 'What we found on the bed was a bag of peppermint creams.'

6

Like an Ugly Little Story by
de Maupassant

Despite the loathing and contempt in which she was generally held, there were a few to whom Mrs. Mansbridge's sudden death brought secret feelings of horror, grief, remorse and guilt — but the one person who was really frightened by it, the flesh walking on the back of her neck whenever she thought of it, was the maid Norah.

Not for a thousand pounds, she maintained, would she remain alone with the doctor in the old stone house; she would be dead scared.

'Well, it was upsetting for you, I grant,' agreed her mother. 'But there's no call to get fanciful and chuck up a good job. What have you got to be scared about?'

'I've no wish to be murdered in my bed,' the girl muttered sullenly.

'Whatever are you talking about, you

great silly? This is what comes of going to the pictures so much, it gives you ideas.'

'People don't die sudden like that for nothing.'

'Well, if you'll take my advice you won't go around calling that poor man a murderer, or you'll find yourself in real trouble, my girl.'

'I know what I know.'

'Then keep your mouth shut and you'll come to no harm.'

'How can I?' the girl wailed. 'I've got to give evidence. I'm a witness, and if they ask me, I'll have to speak the truth, won't I?'

'Oh, how you go on! Just because they had a few words.'

'You didn't see what I saw. Never shall I forget the way he looked when they told him she was dead. It gives me a cold grue to think about it,' she said with a shudder.

'I've told you, shock takes people different ways.'

'It didn't come as no shock to him, you could tell. He couldn't even squeeze out a tear, you can't say that's natural.'

'Doctors don't cry,' averred Mrs. Williams.

'Why not, then? They're human same as us, aren't they?'

'They seen too much of death, that's why. It don't mean no more than seeing a chicken with its head chopped off would to you or me.'

'A person ought to have feelings all the same,' Norah said obstinately.

★　★　★

In the dreadful days between the death and the inquest, Robert Mansbridge occupied himself with the necessary depressing task of sorting through Editha's things. It helped to keep his thoughts at bay. The wastepaper baskets were soon overflowing with torn-up letters and old receipted bills. They had a joint account; and, looking through her cheque-book, he was faintly puzzled to see a blank counterfoil. She had drawn her weekly housekeeping cheque as usual on the day of her death. The blank counterfoil came after that, so it must have been on the same day. He realized that it might well have been a spoiled cheque, but then surely she would have written another. The niggling detail fretted him, till at last he telephoned the bank and asked if a cheque of that serial number had been paid in. It had, and they supplied the details.

The cheque had been made out to Cash and had been drawn the same day. It was for one hundred pounds against their deposit account. Presented by a man, a stranger.

It was in the deposit account that Robert had saved up the money for their annual holiday: it was incredible that Editha should have broached it without telling him. What had become of it? Who was the strange man who had drawn the money out?

It was like some ugly little story by de Maupassant in which, after the wife's death, evidences of her deception are revealed by degrees to the trusting husband.

He was so dazed that he could only stare blankly at Norah when she asked if she might speak to him. The fixed intensity of his gaze completely unnerved her, as if she expected him to hack her to pieces with a cleaver there and then.

She managed at last to stammer out that she wanted to give in her notice, and followed this with some lies about Mum wanting her to come home right away. He didn't seem to believe her when she said her Mum was ill, and of course it was rather a daft thing to have said to a doctor because then he wanted to know just what was wrong with her. So Norah dropped that one and said the fact was that she wanted to make a change.

'First you say one thing, then another,' he complained. 'What is it really?'

She felt herself go red. Really, Mum didn't think it right for her to be alone in the house with a gentleman, it would make people talk. This didn't do either. He dismissed that as nonsense and offered to have a word with her mother on the matter; that was simply too absurd to take seriously, he said.

Norah was not a particularly good servant, but the thought of having to find a substitute for her filled him with dismay. That was all. But it seemed to Norah that he was determined not to let her escape; that, just as she made excuses to leave, he made excuses to keep her. She was bemused with terror; she could think of nothing else to say. Somehow her shaking legs got her out of the room.

⋆   ⋆   ⋆

It was gloriously hot, the sun beaming out of a cloudless sky. The sort of day when it is good to be alive. People greeted one another with smiles and children ran about the streets besmearing their faces with ice-lollies. But inside the village hall it was cold and stuffy, patches of plaster showed unattractively on the green-painted walls, and the high north windows were so grimy that the sky outside looked quite grey.

Mr. Knightley, the solicitor from Cambury, presided as Coroner. He took the police evidence first. The little box of sodium amylobarbitone capsules found in the bathroom cupboard was handed up as an exhibit. (The peppermint creams were found on analysis to be nothing but peppermint creams, and so were not offered as evidence.) The police surgeon described his findings at the post-mortem. The deceased, he found, was suffering from an affliction of the kidneys. In the stomach was a considerable quantity of alcohol, plus six grains of sodium amylobarbitone.

At mention of the sodium amylobarbitone there was a sound throughout the small courtroom like a wind stirring the trees. The Coroner looked up severely, giving a moment for the rustling to subside, before asking whether the amount of sodium amylobarbitone taken was sufficient to cause death.

The police surgeon said cautiously, 'Not necessarily. It is a large amount, but individual idiosyncrasies to a drug can vary enormously. On the other hand, even a normal dose taken in conjunction with alcohol has been sufficient to cause death in a quite healthy person. And the deceased was not healthy; the dangerous reaction of alcohol to the drug was greatly aggravated by the kidney affliction from which she was suffering by delaying the passing of the stomach contents.'

Mr. Knightley's pen scratched industriously.

Next, he wanted to know if it was possible to determine at what time the drug had been taken; how long before death, that is.

There was a rather tedious discussion about this, the police surgeon obviously reluctant to commit himself. The most he would say was that he did not think it could have been later than six p.m., and probably, in this instance, not earlier than two o'clock.

Dr. Horace was then called.

He said he had been sent for by the maid, who was alarmed by the appearance of her mistress. He had got round there soon after ten and found the lady in a deep coma, pulse feeble and irregular, breathing very shallow and slow. In between his efforts to save her life, he naturally tried to get hold of her husband, but he could not find him. They said at the nursing-home that he had left soon after nine, and after that Dr. Horace had not been able to trace him. Despite all he could do, Mrs. Mansbridge died at ten to eleven. Whereupon he telephoned for the police. Dr. Mansbridge arrived about a quarter of an hour after they did.

Then it was Norah Williams' turn.

She was very nervous and spoke in an almost inaudible voice. She returned at half-past nine, she said, and after making herself some tea and stoking the boiler had gone upstairs to turn down the bed and draw the curtains. And then she saw Mrs. Mansbridge on the bed, asleep but not undressed. She thought it a bit funny — queer, that is. She spoke to her, touched her, and then she got frightened and ran downstairs to see if there was a message on the pad where she could find the doctor. She didn't know what was the right thing to do, but at last she got hold of Dr. Horace and asked him if he'd be kind enough to come round as Madam seemed to be ill.

'Well, Mrs. Mansbridge hadn't exactly said she was ill that morning, only that she couldn't be bothered with any lunch and didn't want to be disturbed … Yes, she did particularly say not to tell Dr. Mansbridge … He went up at once … Well, there were words … No, I never heard them exactly quarrel before, I don't think … Well, she said he'd be glad when she was dead. Then he hit her and she cried out … He'd left the bedroom door open, I could hardly help hearing … Well, I couldn't hear everything, only bits here and there … He gave her something to drink, I don't know what, but he came down with the empty glass in his hand ... No, he washed it himself right away. Then he said I could go out if I liked, and I went ... No, Madam had no callers. Not while I was there ... Thank you, sir.' She minced modestly away.

Last of all, Dr. Mansbridge was called. He walked past the people without looking at them to the stand. He might have been unaware of their eyes.

He went patiently through the events of that day. His wife had apparently been in her usual health when he left that morning, so that he had been, yes, surprised, perhaps he could agree, a little perturbed even, when the maid told him that she had retired to her room and did not wish to be disturbed. Naturally, he went up to see what the trouble was. She complained merely of headache. No, she had not seemed quite herself, rather agitated. He looked faintly surprised when he was asked about the quarrel that was said to have taken place.

There was no quarrel, he said; he was simply annoyed to find she had been drinking whisky when she knew how bad it was for her in her condition. She became a little hysterical and he administered a mild bromide and advised her to lie down. There was nothing whatsoever for him to feel in the least anxious about. The maid wanted to go out, so he let her go. After lunch he went to his surgery and attended to his files. He was there till about five and then he had to go out on his evening round. Before he left the house he went up to see his wife and found her asleep, so he had not disturbed her. Clearly her sleep had not appeared in any way unnatural to him or he would not have left her. She had fallen asleep while reading, as anyone might. Yes, that was the last time he saw her alive.

Mr. Knightley said, 'The bromide you gave her was not sodium amylobarbitone?'

'Certainly not.'

'You couldn't have given it to her in error?'

'That is impossible.'

'Had it ever been prescribed for her, by you or any other medical man?'

'No.'

'Will you tell the jury how there came to be some sodium amylobarbitone capsules in the bathroom cupboard?'

'I had put them up for myself several

months ago. At the beginning of the year I was overworked and not sleeping well, so I took them for a few nights to get me back into normal sleeping habits. I'd forgotten they were there.'

'Mrs. Mansbridge would be aware that they were there?'

'Possibly.'

'In this box found by the police, there are three capsules. How many did you take?'

'Two or three, I suppose.'

'How many were there to begin with?'

'I'm afraid I can't recollect. I might only have put up half a dozen.'

'Would that be a usual amount?'

'There is no 'usual' amount in that sense. It depends on the patient. One might make up a dozen, two dozen, fifty … '

'You might have made up a dozen for yourself; you don't remember?'

'I might have, I don't remember.'

'It is not possible to discover the exact amount from your Drug Book?'

Dr. Mansbridge hesitated.

'Unfortunately, there was an accident with the book — some nitric acid was spilled on it and that particular page was among the pages damaged.'

'An unfortunate coincidence indeed,' observed Mr. Knightley drily. He continued writing in silence. Presently he raised his eyes again to ask:

'Dr. Mansbridge, I am obliged to ask you if your wife at any time ever spoke to you about taking her own life?'

The doctor was observed to moisten his lips before replying. 'Sometimes,' he said, 'these last few months.'

'Do you know why?'

'She believed she was suffering from cancer.'

'Did you not attempt to convince her she was mistaken?'

'Repeatedly. She thought I was keeping the truth from her.'

'Did she on any occasion ask you to give her a poison?'

'No. Never.'

'Or discuss methods of killing herself?'

'It never got as far at that.'

'More in the nature of a threat, perhaps?'

'Not at all. It was merely a passing mood evoked by depression.'

'At all events, you did not take the

suggestion seriously?'

'I saw no reason to. The complaint from which she was suffering is often character-ized by attacks of acute depression. If only I could have persuaded her to be more co-operative over her treatment, there would have been nothing to worry about.'

'You did not consider there was any risk in leaving the sodium amylobarbitone cap-sules where she had free access to them?'

'No.'

'And on this last day of her life, did she mention her death to you?'

Dr. Mansbridge frowned.

'Something was said of it, but not in that context.'

'Exactly what was said? You understand that I am trying to discover her state of mind at the time.'

'It was just some foolishness. I'm afraid I was not really paying attention. She was annoyed with me for making a fuss about the whisky.'

'You have told us that you were alone in the house with your wife from two o'clock to five, and we have heard that you left the nursing home soon after nine. And after that you could not be found: will you please tell us where you were from that time until you returned at a quarter past eleven?'

'It was a lovely evening; I went for a walk.'

'For two hours?'

'So it appears. I was not particularly paying attention to the time.'

'Were you alone?'

'I'm afraid I don't see the necessity for that question,' the doctor said stiffly.

'Let me put it another way. Did you during those two hours meet anyone who could corroborate your statement?'

'Yes. I saw Miss Duncton, a patient of mine. In fact, I drove her home before going home myself.'

'How long were you with her?'

'Almost the whole time,' said Dr. Mansbridge with an ironic smile, and for the first time permitted himself one cool glance at the people in the body of the room rustling like doves in immemorial elms, murmuring like innumerable bees. That most uncritical of men was visited by a sudden qualm of distaste. Then he was told to stand down and the coroner began to address the jury.

'We are here to determine how the deceased met her death. There are three possibilities you must bear in mind while considering the evidence. The deceased may have taken the sodium amylobarbitone inadvertently, unaware of its narcotic properties, or unaware of what would constitute a lethal dose: if that is your conclusion you will return a verdict of accidental death. Or, you may conclude that she took the drug and the alcohol with the deliberate intention of taking her own life: in which event you will bring in a verdict of *felo de se* or suicide while the balance of her mind was disturbed. (I will presently explain to you how you are to decide between those similar terms.) Lastly, you may decide that the sodium amylobarbitone was administered by another person or persons, and then you will bring in a verdict of wilful murder.'

He then proceeded to summarize the testimony of the witnesses for their benefit.

★   ★   ★

The foreman — a thin, yellow-faced man with glasses, and a mole on his cheek — stood up and cleared his throat:

'We find the deceased died of an overdose of sodium amylobarbitone. But we do not consider that there is sufficient evidence to determine how it was administered.'

'You wish to return an open verdict?'

'Yes, sir,' he said thankfully.

But no one else was thankful. An open verdict was most unsatisfactory; it left one feeling flat and aggrieved, without an attitude.

The very ambiguity of the verdict lent fresh savour to speculation; the question abided; it remained a matter for fascinated conjecture.

Down in the cottages by the railway embankment, Mrs. Posset was discussing it over the fence with her neighbour as they hung out the washing.

'Well, I ask you. How could anyone take a whole lot of pills and not know they done it? Accident, I'll never believe. Of course she must have took them deliberate and put the box back in the cupboard so that no one would guess.'

'But whatever for?' said Mrs. Tidy, ducking between the sopping sheets to argue the point. 'What's a lady like her got to kill herself about? Folks like her never go short of nothing, even when they're what they call broke. Not like us poor sods,' she added cheerfully, 'as sometimes don't know where their next meal is coming from.' (Mrs. Tidy was always dragging in a piece about how hard up she was, though what she did with all the money she earned was a mystery; she never seemed to have a penny in her pocket, and was forever borrowing half-a-crown for the insurance man or a shilling for the gas.)

Mrs. Posset, with her mouth full of pegs, looked down her nose.

'Of course,' Mrs. Tidy went on, 'if a person's in real debt and don't see no way out — like my poor Freddy's sister who stuck her head in the gas oven because she just couldn't stick the worry of it any longer; or like some poor silly kid who's got herself in some trouble with some boy — well, that's different. You can understand it. But people like her can't have any real worries that I can see.'

'Here,' said Mrs. Posset, coming to lean

her thick arms upon the fence, 'haven't you heard, then?'

'Heard what?'

'They say the reason why she done it was on account of his carryings-on.'

'Him! Never!' cried Mrs. Tidy in a tone that plainly contradicted her denial. 'Who's he been carrying on with, then?'

'Ah, that I can't say,' Mrs. Posset said austerely, as though she could tell if she would but had sworn never to divulge it.

'I can't see me killing myself for a man,' Mrs. Tidy scoffed. 'I'd show him a thing or two pretty quick if he tried anything funny with me, you can take my word!'

'Ah, so she did, if it's to be believed what I hear! I had it from Mrs. Williams herself.' She leaned nearer. 'And her daughter said that that was the very thing they was having words about that day. He was asking her to divorce him.'

'Go on!'

'True as I'm standing here. And she came over a bit acid, nasty-like, and that was when he knocked her down.'

'You don't say! Well, fancy — the doctor! And him always so quiet and pleasant-spoken,' Mrs. Tidy said wonderingly.

'Mrs. Williams said her daughter wouldn't stay on there now for a million pounds.'

Mrs. Tidy clicked her tongue.

'What he must be feeling like now: I wouldn't have his conscience!' she declared.

'Men ain't got no consciences that I ever discovered,' Mrs. Posset said grimly.

⋆ ⋆ ⋆

Colonel Fitzalan, bending at the knees to brush his hair before the glass, said, 'Is she meant to have taken those damned capsules that old Robert said he put up for himself, or not?'

'I don't suppose we shall ever know,' his wife murmured as she struggled into her old skirt.

'That was a bad error of judgment Robert made, in my opinion, destroying that page in his Drug Book. A damned silly thing to do.'

'You think he did it deliberately?'

'People will say he did. You know how they talk.'

'People will always talk; we're talking ourselves,' his wife said mildly.

'That's only between ourselves; there's no harm in that. After all, we're friends of his. Unless we know where we are, it's going to be hard to stand up for him to other people.'

'I honestly can't see what he can have hoped to prove by it — or, rather, what he *didn't* want proved,' said his wife, heaving the skirt round her plump body till it was roughly in the right position. 'It makes me feel like Alice in Wonderland. I can't make out whether it was to make us think she *had* taken them or that she *hadn't.* Anything with figures always does confuse me so.'

Her husband grunted and clapped the brushes together.

He said slowly, 'If there were only six pills originally in that little box they found, and Robert had taken three, so that three were left, that means that Editha got hers somewhere else — or they were somehow administered to her by someone else without her knowing.'

'Why, Henry!' Mrs. Fitzalan said with a nervous laugh. 'Editha could be very disagreeable, but I simply can't believe that anyone would want to kill the poor woman.'

The Colonel was hitching himself into his jacket and didn't answer. At last he said, 'I dare say no one would ever have thought of it if Robert hadn't tried to cover up. Doesn't look well. Gives people ideas. Can't understand a chap like Robert doing such a stoopid thing.'

'But, Henry *dear*,' said his wife, turning from the dressing-table to stare at him, 'that would mean that Robert believed it was murder ... and ... and was *condoning it*! He'd never do a thing like that! Especially when it was his own wife.' She stared in amazement at the foolish-looking woman in the glass with her mouth full of hairpins. Behind her in the mirror, Henry's expression was very odd — almost, she would have said, *guilty.* She said aloud, 'Unless you mean that you think it was Robert who killed her?'

'No, no, no! Of course not,' shouted the Colonel. 'Good God!' he exclaimed, snatching out of his breast pocket the handkerchief he had just so neatly folded and wiping his brow. Women had the most devilish way of putting things!

'Ready for breakfast, dear?' said his wife.

'Quite,' said the Colonel heavily.

★ ★ ★

'No one could be fonder of Robert than I am,' declared Mrs. Ambrose over the dinner table, 'but of course it was an absolute disaster that he should have been with that girl — even if they were only walking in the wood — on that particular night. I do honestly think he's been frightfully foolish over the whole affair — I mean the affair with Miss D. I've said that all along, haven't I?' she appealed to her husband, who mumbled that he didn't think it was a fit subject for discussion.

'Now, don't be stuffy,' she begged. 'It's not *sub judice,*' she added, with a merry laugh. 'And anyway, we're all friends of Robert's here.'

'As a matter of fact,' said Mr. Lawrence, 'it was really rather a snip for Robert that he was out with this — this lady-friend of his; it is not a thing he would have done if he had known his wife was dying.'

'Oh, is that how it strikes you?' Mrs. Ambrose said earnestly. 'Yes, I do see what you mean. How interesting!' She smiled and, much to her husband's relief, promptly changed the subject.

★　★　★

'My dear, it's exactly like the Crippen case,' Miss Lucas confided to her crony Miss Barnaby, leaning across the table in the darkest corner of The Warming Pan, where Everyone who was Anyone congregated daily for morning coffee. There, one saw all one's friends without any of the bother and expense of entertaining. For ladies with not much to do, it was a delightful way to pass the morning, in that most dangerous of innocent occupations — gossip. And with the inquest still fresh in all their minds ...

Mulling it over to herself, Miss Lucas had been struck by its pointed resemblance to the Crippen case. She was old enough to remember the excitement of that: this was even better, being so near home. How marvellously thrilling, she could not help thinking, if she should be the one, the first one to see the connection, to stir up public opinion, to make the police realize what they must look for, to give evidence at the trial … She saw herself at the Old Bailey, with a calm smile on her lips, defeating the purpose of opposing counsel's questions, making nonsense of their whole line of defence …

Miss Lucas's remark had quite taken Miss Barnaby's breath away with all its implications. Miss Lucas was so downright and convinced of her own judgment that too hasty a show of incredulity would only offend her, so Miss Barnaby chewed the suggestion with her scone in meditative silence for some minutes.

'But, I mean, he didn't, you know … chop up her body and try to hide it,' she ventured at length.

'However, he is a doctor,' Miss Lucas pointed out triumphantly, glancing over her shoulder to make sure she could not be overheard. 'Crippen, too, was a quiet little man whom everybody liked and felt sorry for because his wife bullied him. Crippen, too, had a timid, inconspicuous girl in love with him. If it hadn't been for Ethel le

Neve, he might never have been driven to it; but he wanted to marry her. You see?'

Miss Barnaby was staggered by her friend's brilliant exposition. Such a clear-cut brain! It came, no doubt, from having been a school teacher. She could only gaze at her admiringly.

Miss Lucas nodded.

'Possibly there are reasons why our doctor should want to marry you-know-who.'

'You mean ... ' breathed Miss Barnaby, and fell agaping at this thought. 'But wouldn't a doctor know ... I mean, there are ways of ... '

'Oh, yes, a doctor would know ... But supposing he wanted the child, having none of his own? That would be reason enough, I should think.'

'But such a *wicked* thing to do,' Miss Barnaby murmured, unconsenting yet to such a crime. 'Why not, I mean, simply have got a divorce?'

'In the first place, his wife may have refused to divorce him. And in the second, people are so funny in their ideas about respectability, aren't they? Doctors are like parsons and lawyers; it wouldn't be thought at all the thing for them to be divorced.'

Miss Barnaby nodded thoughtfully like a China mandarin. An involuntary shudder seized her, and, hunching herself together, she leaned forward.

'But what are we going to do?' she asked. 'It does seem to me that somebody ought to do something. He oughtn't to be let get away with it. I mean, if he really did … '

'Oh, we won't let him get away with it,' said Miss Lucas, her assurance so martial, so positively Amazonian, that it was quite sinister. Miss Barnaby shivered again and wondered if she could have caught a cold.

7

The Old Stone House Seemed
Curiously Empty

Dr. Mansbridge could hardly have been unaware of the talk going on. One had only to see the way people talking in the street turned on him a quick masking smile, like malicious children caught by the teacher at their plotting, to know instinctively that they were discussing Mrs. Mansbridge's death. It would have been foolish to expect it could be otherwise in a place where what one's neighbour purchased at the fishmonger's was of more moment than the day's headlines of disaster. Not realizing the trend of their thoughts, Robert believed that in time, in a few days, the subject would become dull and used-up, and some fresh scandal would take its place.

What he needed was a rush of work. He would have been grateful for an epidemic to keep him from thinking; but, strangely enough, he had less to do than usual. People were perhaps respecting his bereavement, feeling he should be left alone for a while, given time to get over it. He seemed to have dropped into a deep pool of silence, as if intimations of his grief had sealed him off from the world, like a stuffed bird enclosed in a glass bell, its beady eyes pathetically simulating life.

Once Norah had gone and he was left alone, the old stone house seemed curiously empty, so comfortless and desolate that each time he dreaded afresh to return to it. One evening, unable to bear the stillness any longer, he walked over to The King's Head for a drink and the solace of a more companionable atmosphere.

He scarcely ever went to pubs — it did not do for doctors to frequent such places — and this was almost the first time he had entered one in his own village. Perhaps that was why everyone stopped and turned to stare as he came in. The cheerful racket ceased in the brightly-lit saloon with its warm beery smell, and they stood arrested in surprise like some absurd *tableau vivant.* Then the awkward moment passed and he was greeted politely by this one and that. Yet, as he advanced to the bar, he had the odd impression that they were not so much making room for him as actually drawing away, as though he earned about him some chill graveyard air.

The landlord came forward with a solemn mien, ill-suited to his gross good-humoured face, to take the doctor's order. The darts players continued with their game, but more quietly now, as though in a hurry to be finished with it. There was no more laughter, and all the talk had died to a subdued murmuring. He had the idea that his presence embarrassed them. The landlord nodded soberly at his few remarks. No one else spoke to him. Perhaps they were shocked at seeing him in such a place so soon after his wife's funeral. Perhaps they merely did not like to intrude on the days conventionally allotted to his grief. Well, the experiment was not a success, and he did not feel inclined to repeat it. It had the effect of making him feel lonelier, more cut off, than ever.

Somewhere inside him, such incidents left a bruised feeling. Liking people himself, in his cheerful, moderate way, he had supposed they liked him too, had believed himself to be popular. It seemed he had been mistaken.

Sitting alone night after night in that dreary house, stubbornly dragging his thoughts away from the dark groove they persistently retraced; trying to read, trying to listen to the radio, but seeing on the printed page only his own predicament, hearing in the music only the echo of his own despair ...

He told himself harshly that he must make an effort, must somehow pick up the threads of life again. Since his friends seemed so oddly chary of disturbing his sad solitude, he would have to be the one to make the first move. The Ambroses, now, and old Lawrence, and perhaps the Fitzalans, he must ask them round. 'A little dinner ... and bridge,' he thought vaguely, but at once was struck by the hopelessness of such a scheme. The task of organizing the affair, without anyone to cook the meal and serve it, was beyond him. He wondered dimly how he had managed such affairs when he was a bachelor. Now, glancing about, he noticed for the first time the dead flowers, cobwebs in the comer, curtains pulled back not quite straight. He *must* take steps to find a housekeeper who would know how to look after things. Then it would be possible to ask people in again. Even apart from the pleasures of entertaining, he could not go on with just a scrubbing-woman to do for him. The old woman got his breakfast, tidied his bed, and doddled around, but that was not good enough for a doctor's establishment. Tomorrow he would set about getting a housekeeper.

★   ★   ★

Two days before the end of term, Janet Scott found herself alone for a moment in the Common Room with Edward Golding.

'You're looking very pleased with life,' she commented with a smile. 'What's the news?'

He hit himself on the chest with mock pride and smiled back at her.

'Bets is going to have a child.'

'Well, congratulations!' she cried. 'When is it to be?'

'Next March, we think.' He put his finger to his lips. 'You're the first person we've told. So mum's the word.'

She laughed. 'Mum is indeed the word. Is Bets pleased about it? I don't need to ask if you are!' For his eyes were shining with such happiness that she could not bear to meet them.

'Ah, she's thrilled. Bless her!'

'So everything's all right again.'

'How do you mean?' he said, puzzled. 'Ah, that! Good Lord, yes. She's forgotten all about it.' He could hardly have told Janet more plainly how completely unimportant his old affair with her had become to him and his Betsy than by the utter indifference with which he dismissed it. He said enthusiastically, 'Jan, you must be the boy's godmother.'

Janet laughed.

'Thanks for the compliment! But I hardly think that would do, you know.'

'Why not?'

She wondered that he could be so dense. But if he could not see why, she was certainly not going to tell him. She said, 'I'm not a godmotherly sort of person, I'm afraid. I wouldn't know how to guide his little feet into the paths of righteousness. You must have some rich friend who could be of use to him later. I couldn't even afford him a silver mug, poor poppet. You must do better than that for your firstborn.'

'What nonsense!'

'Besides,' she said quickly, 'I may not be here. You haven't heard my news yet.' She gave him a brilliant smile. 'I shan't be coming back next term.'

He raised his eyebrows.

'Oh? How's that?'

'I've just given in my notice,' she lied.

'Good for you! Got a better post, I suppose.'

'No. It was just ... oh, I can't stand this place any longer! I feel I've got to get away!' she cried passionately.

'Jolly sensible,' he agreed in his cool, judicious way. 'And with your qualifications it should be easy enough to find another post. Probably a better one, at that.'

'I'm not going to try for another teaching job. It's so damnably stultifying!'

He took out his pouch and began filling his pipe.

'Mmm? What shall you do, then?'

'I don't know yet. So long as it has nothing to do with painting, I don't care what it is.'

'But my good girl ... ' he protested with a laugh.

'What?'

'Well, what else can you do? I didn't know you had any other skills.'

She said drily, 'My dear Ned, you must think me singularly incompetent if you imagine I couldn't turn my hand to anything else. I could get a job tomorrow as a cook.'

'Oh, if that's all your ambition; I agree.'

'It's just because I am so ambitious as a painter that I'm not going to waste my talent teaching scruffy little boys how to draw pots.'

He flicked the spent match into the empty grate.

'Ah, now I'm with you,' he said, round the pipe clenched between his teeth. 'It's the school you're tired of. Not necessarily us.'

'Us?' she said lightly. She had already hopelessly committed her future by this crazy impulse to see how he would react if he learnt that she was going. All she longed for was one word to show that, however much he tried to hide it, he still felt something for her, would be even ever so faintly reluctant to lose her altogether. She said, with a sardonic smile, 'Who is 'us'?' hoping to drive him to an admission.

'You have a great many friends in the village, haven't you? Won't you miss them if you go away?'

She shrugged.

'What on earth could I find to do here?'

'They say Dr. Mansbridge wants a housekeeper.'

'Oh, thanks awfully. How delightful that would be!'

'You said you only wanted a job as cook. Looking after a single gent is supposed to be a snip. After his martyrdom with the late and terribly-*un*lamented Mrs. Mansbridge, he'd probably fall for a nice girl like you hook, line and sinker. Widowers are the easiest of all to catch, they say.'

She flushed darkly.

If his words had been motivated by spite, she could have forgiven him and even been gratified by this evidence of his desire to hurt her; but they were said in such a good-humoured way that she knew he had not meant to humiliate her — and nothing could be more humiliating than that. What could be more offensive than to advise one's discarded mistress to catch herself another man? It may have been only a clumsy jest, but only someone utterly insensitive and obtuse could have made it. She could never forgive him for it.

In that instant, all her affection for him seemed to curdle inside her. She was swept through with hatred and contempt, as much for her own delusion as for him. It disgusted her to think she could ever have suffered over anyone so crude and stupid, so conceited as to be downright ridiculous. How could she have been taken in for a minute by such a dense, pompous ass? she wondered scornfully. He and his Betsy were well suited; poor simpleton, she would never have the brain to see through him, and so they would live happy ever after.

Janet moved across the room, with the swaying motion that had once made him liken her to a flower yielding to the breeze, and collected her papers. Then she turned on him her coolest, most tantalizing smile, and said quite mildly:

'What an extraordinary suggestion, Ned. I wonder what on earth gave you the impression that I am out to *catch* a man — whatever that means. It sounds as though you thought one had to run after a man to catch him. I've never run after a man in my life. I can't imagine I ever should. But if I did, I can assure you, my dear, that I wouldn't be interested in second-hand goods.' And with a sweet, false laugh, she skipped out of the room.

* * *

In the old Georgian house with bow windows in the High Street, the atmosphere was heavy with gloom. With Crispin wrapped in a harsh silence, Naomi crept about afraid to speak.

When the news of Editha's death came to them, Naomi, all her jealousy forgotten in an uprush of pity for her friend, had gone to Crispin with outstretched arms. And Crispin, with a stony face, had pushed her away and mounted alone to her room. The moment that might have brought them together had cleft them apart.

Crispin did not weep for Editha, and her name was never mentioned between them; but whenever they were together Editha was there too, haunting them like a ghost — a jeering ghost, that spoke of her triumph to Naomi and reminded Crispin of her defeat.

Only the merest bread-and-butter things could be mentioned without rousing thoughts of the dead woman. The two avoided one another's eyes. Crispin was matter-of-fact; Naomi subdued. To watch Crispin muffled into her arid grief made her feel oddly guilty. It was dreadful not to know what she was thinking. Naomi had the silly notion that in some way Crispin held her to blame for Editha's death and it made her cringe inside.

Had Editha's death been natural, Crispin's attitude might have been very different, but she could not get away from the mysterious circumstances surrounding it. She needed desperately to talk about it with someone — but not with Ryder, she could not bear to speak of it to Ryder. Yet there was one other person who must be feeling as she felt, one other person whose sense of loss was comparable to her own. Their mutual loss created, in her mind, a bond of sympathy between them. She forgot that she had always despised him; all her detestation was wiped out.

A south-westerly gale rattled the windows of the old stone house, gusts of rain trickling like tears down the panes. The house looked unspeakably dreary, as if it had been deserted for years. The trees sighed round the house, their bending branches ushering the wind first this way and then that, the leaves clattering stiffly together in protest. Roses hung dejected and sodden, scattering their petals in sudden bursts over the path. The desolation was reflected in Dr. Mansbridge's face as he approached his home. It was the sort of day when one longs for the comfort of a leaping fire and a fat brown teapot warming on the hearth, and there would be neither for him. Wearily, he let himself into the house and found Miss Crispin waiting for him in the cold drawing-room. He almost showed his surprise in his face.

She was standing in the middle of the room with a feverishly tense expression.

'Won't you sit down?' he said politely. He rubbed his cold hands together and looked vaguely round, but the fire was unlaid.

Crispin walked over to the empty grate, turned her back on it and locked her hands behind her.

She said abruptly, 'You are wondering why I have come to see you.'

'Not a professional visit, I take it.'

'I wanted to speak to you.' She stopped, as if the words baulked at being thrust out of her mouth. He watched her with his detached professional gaze. 'About — Editha,' she added with difficulty.

'Oh, yes?' he said pleasantly. 'You were a friend of hers, I believe.'

She walked over to the window and stared out at the garden's trees tossing in grief. It took her a moment to control her lips. She pressed her fingers against her mouth, and gazed beyond the blurred pane.

'I want to know how she died,' she said at last.

'It seems that is something we shall never know,' said Dr. Mansbridge.

At that she turned, angered at his quiet, complacent tone.

'And are you satisfied with that?' she cried, thrusting her shaking fists deep into her pockets. 'Because I'm not.'

Dr. Mansbridge said, but quite inoffensively:

'Forgive me, but I fail to see what business it is of yours.'

She said, on a note of rage and contempt:

'It is the business of every decent person to see that justice is done to the dead!'

'Justice?' he repeated wonderingly, eyeing her with one brow raised in an expression that reminded her oddly of his dead wife.

'Yes, justice,' she asserted. 'Apparently you are content to leave your wife's memory under this ugly cloud.'

'I'm afraid I am very dense, but I don't seem to understand,' he said on a frigid note.

Crispin raked her hair with her lean fingers. She was making a muck of it, with her ungovernable passion for justice — for a justice never obtainable in this world. The last thing she wanted was to put him against her. She needed his co-operation. Till now, she had not supposed she would have to win his help; rather, she had taken it for granted that he would welcome her support and succinct argument. She began awkwardly to apologize — always a difficult role for her.

'We must not quarrel.' She made a gesture towards him with her hand. 'I only want ... '

'Suppose we sit down, then,' he offered with a shadowy smile.

She would have preferred to continue restlessly pacing the room, but she seated herself unwillingly on the edge of an arm of one of the chairs. She leaned towards him, her strained blue eyes willing him to sincerity.

'Let us be frank with one another, Dr. Mansbridge: you must know that she could never have taken that stuff by mistake?'

He took out his cigarette-case and offered it to her. She shook her head. He lit his own cigarette and blew out a cloud of smoke before he answered.

'If it happened, it *could* have happened; but I admit I don't know how it could have occurred.'

'It would have to mean that she mistook

the capsules for something else, wouldn't it? How could she? Those capsules are quite unmistakable. Aren't they?' she pressed him.

'Suppose I agree that it couldn't have been an accident,' Dr. Mansbridge said quietly. 'Do you understand that the alternatives are suicide or murder?'

'I don't accept the idea of suicide,' Crispin said quickly. 'I am certain as I've ever been of anything that your wife didn't kill herself.'

'Oh? May one ask what makes you so sure?'

'I know it,' she said, watching him.

He said lightly, 'From evidence? Or merely inner conviction?'

Unsmiling, Crispin said, 'Inner conviction is evidence too — evidence based on one's knowledge of the person's character.'

He said in the same, almost jesting, tone: 'And when such convictions about the character conflict, what then?'

'Meaning that you knew Editha better than I did?'

'She was my wife,' he pointed out. 'One can hardly live with a person for eighteen years without learning a little about them.'

Such ridiculous assurance was enough to make her smile if she had not been in such desperate earnest.

She said harshly:

'And *you* think she killed herself?'

He said coldly, 'All that was gone into at the inquest. I do not propose to go over it again.' But she fancied that his hand shook as he pressed out his cigarette.

'I shall never believe it,' she cried, knotting her bony hands together. 'Never!'

'Then let us leave it at that, shall we?' he said with an air of relief, getting to his feet.

Crispin stood up too, but not to take her leave.

'No,' she said. 'I won't leave it at that. I can't. I must know.' She looked at him boldly. 'Why don't you want to discuss it with me? What are you afraid of finding out?'

'Afraid?' he said, astonished. 'Has it not occurred to you that the subject is painful to me? It is particularly distasteful to talk of with a stranger. I'm sorry,' he added in a dismissive manner.

'I'm sorry, too,' she said, 'that you should

regard me as merely prying and impertinent. I too find it painful … It is only because I was so fond of your wife … ' She turned abruptly away and went over to the window, biting her lip. 'Surely it is more painful still not to know the truth?' she said after a while.

'The truth?' he said wryly.

She turned, and their eyes met in a long, steady glance like wrestlers struggling for supremacy.

'You would prefer to believe that she committed suicide,' Crispin said incredulously. 'Well, I will swear before God she never did. Only the day before, she was making plans for the future.'

He went so far as to say, 'Many suicides do the same. It is a well-known psychological projection.'

'Oh, my God, is it possible that you really believe such nonsense yourself?' she cried contemptuously. 'Are you telling me that after you had left her quietly lying down, she got up again and went to the bathroom, took six capsules — and why then didn't she take the whole lot? That's what suicides generally do, isn't it? They want to be sure of taking enough to make a good job of it, so at least I've always understood. However, she didn't. She took only six, and then carefully put the other three back in the box and the box into the cupboard, and then went back to her room, lay down on the bed again, and went on reading her book and eating sweets as though nothing had happened? Was that just psychological projection too?' she scornfully asked.

He said flatly, 'It is simply a possibility that cannot be dismissed without further evidence. If it had not been so, doubtless a different verdict would have been returned.'

Crispin said, 'What is conclusive evidence? I had a letter from her written on the day she died.' She cast a quick defiant glance sideways at him. 'I wouldn't betray her confidence even now if I didn't feel obliged to show you that she couldn't have been contemplating suicide. She wrote asking me to lend her some money.'

'Yes?' Dr. Mansbridge said politely towards the austere profile silhouetted against the window. 'She wanted to borrow a hundred pounds, I suppose?'

This time it was Crispin who was taken

aback.

'Then you knew?'

Dr. Mansbridge regarded the nails on his left hand.

'Did she happen to mention why she wanted it?' he asked in a carefully indifferent voice.

Crispin shook her head.

'No. But that's neither here nor there. What it does show is that death couldn't have been in her thoughts — or why ask for money? If I had refused her ... But she was dead before I received the letter. So it wasn't despair, was it?'

Dr. Mansbridge drummed his fingers impatiently against the side of his chair.

'But, my dear lady, to what is all this leading?'

She said in surprise, 'Why, just this: if she didn't take an overdose of the barbiturate deliberately, and she didn't take it by mistake ... what is left?'

'Only murder,' he said in an even tone.

'Only murder,' she gravely repeated.

With a tired attempt at irony, Dr. Mansbridge said, 'You regard that as a preferable alternative?'

'No. But I happen to believe it is the truth.'

He said sharply, 'Very well. Now I will ask you a question. Why should anyone have wanted to murder my wife?'

Crispin made a small helpless gesture.

'If we knew the answer to that, there would be no problem.'

'Who is there,' he persisted, 'in this quiet little village full of the most ordinary and respectable people, who could possibly have wanted her out of the way?' He got up and fumbled along the chimney shelf for the matches. He stood there, leaning one elbow on the shelf, and rocked the fender slightly with his foot. 'Can't you see how utterly incredible the idea is?'

'Disagreeable, but not incredible.'

'Editha hadn't an enemy in the world.' The match flickered in his fingers and he bent his head to meet it.

'That's not true. We all of us have enemies, even the saints among us. There were many people who disliked Editha.'

'Oh, come, Miss Crispin!' he said with a faint laugh. 'Now you are talking like a schoolgirl. Backbiting and ill-nature, you know, don't lead to murder.'

She flushed.

'You are being wilfully obtuse. I suppose because you are trying to shirk your responsibility.'

'What do you want me to do?' he said, carefully knocking his ash into the empty grate.

'Find the murderer.'

He looked up, startled, to meet her stony blue eyes.

'What do you mean?'

'Find the murderer,' she repeated, watching him.

He was caught between irritation and an insensate desire to laugh. He rubbed a hand across his face. The woman was fantastic!

'But, my dear Miss Crispin ... really, you talk as if this was some fatuous detective story in which I am to be the prancing amateur nosing behind the scenes. In real life such people do not exist, I assure you.'

'You consider it a matter for mockery?' she coldly said.

'If I took your suggestion seriously, I'm afraid it would make me angry.'

'Why should it?' she said in the same icy tone.

'Miss Crispin, I am a very hard-worked doctor. What time do you suppose I have for such nonsense? You really expect me to go out looking for a murderer in whose existence I scarcely believe? I'm afraid I wouldn't have a clue how to go about it, in any sense of the word.'

'You jump ahead of me. I never suggested you should search for the murderer yourself. That would be foolish indeed,' she said with a sarcastic smile.

'What do you mean then?'

'You could go to the police and tell them that you are not satisfied.'

'So far as the police are concerned, the case is closed.'

'Tell them to open it again. If they won't, go over their heads to Scotland Yard.'

He stared at her. With a feeling of exhaustion, he thought, *But this woman is dangerous!*

'Of course I shall do no such thing,' he assured her decisively. 'If you knew my wife as well as you say, you would know that there could be nothing she would more bitterly resent than a squalid inquiry built round her name. She would not care to have her memory perpetuated like that, believe me, as a sordid subject for investigation in the criminal courts with all its malicious interpretation of past acts.'

'I think it is yourself you are considering,' Crispin said slyly.

'Yes, that too,' he agreed. 'It has all been quite painful enough for me. It does a doctor no good to be talked about ... all this conjecture ... ' He made a gesture. 'Nothing anyone can discover will make any difference. It will not bring Editha back.'

'We see it differently. Perhaps that's inevitable,' she said, buttoning her jacket.

'Yes.' He held the door open for her, and as she passed through it, he said, 'If you propose to make amateur investigations yourself, you might begin at home.'

She halted and said stiffly:

'What do you mean?'

With a cool little bow, Dr. Mansbridge said, 'Ask the friend you live with what she was doing here on the morning my wife died.'

'I don't understand. What could she have

been doing?'

'I've no idea,' he said pleasantly. 'Only, I saw her face as she left, and it was not the face of a woman who had merely been paying a friendly call.'

* * *

Each time that Ryder became aware of Crispin's puzzled gaze resting on her, she found herself looking away uneasily: an apprehension that communicated itself to Crispin; it did seem almost as though Ryder had something to conceal.

Ryder, fidgeting in her chair, at last looked up from the book of silver marks she was studying to ask: 'Is anything the matter?'

Crispin said casually, 'No. What should be?'

'You keep staring at me.'

'Do I?' said Crispin, intent on piercing the end of a cigar. 'I suppose I must have been wondering,' she said, with a rapid glance from the corner of her eye at the other woman, 'why you never mentioned that you went to see Editha before she died.'

She watched the colour drain out of Ryder's face, leaving it like old parchment.

'Why should I have?' she muttered, looking down at her book, marking the place with her finger.

'I really can't see why not. It would seem the normal thing to have spoken of it.'

'There was nothing to say.'

'Then, all the more reason. If there was nothing to hide.'

'Since you made it perfectly plain that you did not want to discuss Editha with me, the opportunity never arose, I simply avoided speaking of it.'

Crispin gave a dry laugh.

'I fancy there must have been rather more to it than that.'

Naomi closed her book and gripped it tightly.

'Exactly what do you mean?'

'It does strike me as excessively curious that you should have gone there on *that* day when you had never been there before. That in itself is surely odd enough, without concealing it from me and — ' She carefully broke the ash of her cigar into the lacquer bowl. ' — the police.'

Naomi sprang from her chair.

'Now what are you hinting at?' she cried. 'Why on earth should I have told the police?'

'You can't really be so stupid,' Crispin said, observing her agitation. 'It must be perfectly obvious that everything which occurred on that day would be of importance to those who were concerned in finding out the truth.'

'You would like to think … How utterly … ' Naomi stuttered incoherently. 'No, I really can't … '

'How you jump to conclusions! It's quite laughable.'

'It is you who is jumping to conclusions,' Naomi interrupted fiercely.

'My dear, I only want to help. Don't you see?'

'No.'

Crispin said, 'Don't you understand, if I can learn about it quite by chance, so may other people? If I think your secrecy strange, what are other people going to think?' She slipped the great cornelian over her knuckle and stared at the light through it. 'Can't you see, my poor child, the very real danger you are in?'

'You are trying to frighten me,' Naomi said in a flat voice, leaning her shaking hands on the table. She stared across at Crispin, trying to decipher her expression through the column of light which rose through the top of the lampshade. Crispin's hair gleamed in the shadows beyond the lamp's mellow circle as she turned her head. 'It's quite senseless, because I have nothing to be afraid of. Nothing at all. You are letting your imagination run away with you.'

'Yes,' agreed the other, 'that is what I am afraid of: other people's imaginations. We should at least,' she went on smoothly, 'concoct a feasible story to tell. Why, for instance, did you go there in the first place?'

'You know why,' Naomi said in a low tone, 'you must know very well. It was about you; because you were leaving me, you said.' She averted eyes dazzled to tears from that luminous golden shaft and stared blindly down at the polished tabletop, cool against her damp hands. Naomi swallowed. 'I wanted at all costs to stop her ... to stop her going away with you ... That's all,' she added after a moment, affected by the utter stillness of the other woman.

Crispin repeated very quietly, 'At all costs to stop her ... ?'

'No, of course not! Not like that! What are you thinking?' Naomi cried in terror, running round to seize those strong beloved hands. 'It wasn't like that at all.' She enunciated with difficulty, 'I went to plead with her ... to beg her ... I knew she was hard and selfish, but I could not believe she knew what it meant ... '

'And then?' Crispin pursued in a light unreal voice.

'Why, nothing. I never saw her. At the last minute, on the doorstep itself, I couldn't go through with it. I ... I can't explain what I felt, you'd never understand ... '

'It's not a very good story, Naomi,' Crispin said, withdrawing herself from her and standing up.

'It's not meant to be judged as a story: it's the truth,' she said, wondering to hear Crispin use her Christian name.

'The point is, will anyone believe it?'

'What do I care whether they do or not,' Naomi said recklessly, 'so long as you believe me ... You do believe me, don't you?'

she said as no reassurance came from the figure in motionless silhouette against the dusky pane. 'Don't you?' she repeated, with beating heart.

But the silent figure made no answer.

8

A Quiet, Respectable Widow

Despite the resolution to find himself a housekeeper, Dr. Mansbridge never did take any active steps to get anyone. He had only the vaguest notion how one was supposed to go about it, and a kind of lethargy descended on him which made all problems equally distasteful, so that he was reluctant to make the effort. He came to rely feebly on the superstitious idea that the right person would somehow present herself at the right time.

And someone did come. A Mrs. Thrale: a quiet, respectable lady in her early fifties, widowed a year and left with small means, so that for the first time in her life she was obliged to go out to work in order to eke out her little income. It was a come-down, of course, and sad at her time of life to have no home, but she knew her misfortune was not unique and she had a little plan to comfort herself with. She had many friends in the village, and the vicar's wife, with whom she was staying, was an old chum from her schooldays. Naturally, she could not expect to stay with her indefinitely, and a little housekeeping job like this would just suit her while she hunted around for some tiny cottage modest enough to suit her needs and her sadly diminished pocket. Such places, she knew, were hard to find nowadays and required much time and patience, but sooner or later something would turn up for her. All her friends were roped in to the hunt. She would not have to work for ever, she inwardly assured herself.

The interview was short. Most of the questions were asked by her. Dr. Mansbridge was so inexperienced in this line of country that he could not remember the right things to ask, and he did not re-alize till much later the many details which should have been agreed between them before a decision was made. But he was too thankful that someone so suitable should have turned up for him to make difficulties. He liked her manner, quiet and assured. He was relieved when she said that she would manage everything without bothering him, but if there was anything he didn't like, he must be sure to tell her; she was there to make him comfortable. Obviously she was going to be the sort of housekeeper everyone hopes for.

He was taken aback the first day to find the table laid for two.

'Who's that for?' he said abruptly.

She flushed prettily.

'Oh, shouldn't I have laid for myself there? Was that where your wife used to sit?' she said, dropping her voice respectfully; and then, with a quick look at him, added: 'Or did you mean you would like me to have my meals in the kitchen? I'm sorry, I didn't think,' she said, beginning to pick up the silver.

But put like that it did sound horribly snobbish and unreasonable. After all, she was a lady, and perhaps could not be expected to eat in that dingy basement kitchen. Although it was the last thing he wanted, to have some strange woman sitting opposite to him day after day with the terrible prospect of conversation, he found himself saying gruffly, 'No, no, of course not. It's quite all right. I just forgot for the moment ... '

At least the woman could cook, and that was more than something. She did know how to make a man comfortable. And somehow she contrived to keep up a flow of dainty talk that required so little response from him that he was able to retire into his own thoughts. In a queer sort of way, it was not altogether unpleasant to have someone there again.

The house once more took on an inhabited air: silver and brass glinted in the corners, and there were fresh flowers in all the rooms. If it had not been for his deep and bewildered sense of loneliness, he could almost have found contentment in this new life. But still his practice insensibly decreased, his patients drifting away from him without a word of explanation. Perhaps there was no explanation that they could give. But, as if he were somehow to blame for this silent drifting away, he was filled with shame. The house became for him a sort of refuge, a place in which to hide from the glances of the curious, somewhere to pass unremarked the hours of idleness. He got even to feel guilty when he had to face Mrs. Thrale again after only a couple of hours' absence, fancying he read contempt in her eyes — or, worse, an open sympathy.

There were moments when he considered selling the practice — while there was still a practice to sell — and getting right away from this place with all its ugly associations. To leave the past behind him and start again somewhere else. Another part of the country, where he was unknown. Or leave England altogether. Sign on as a ship's doctor and see something of the world; travel, and forget. He had had a notion to be a ship's doctor before even he married: it had seemed a fascinatingly easy way of going about the world, and it still held something of its charm for him. It was not too late, he was not too old to enjoy it — hardly in the prime of his life, he thought, with a twist of the lips. Well, now he could go if he liked, there was nothing to prevent it.

Nothing except a queer, stubborn reluctance to let himself be driven out. Nothing except an angry determination not to be beaten; they should not think he had run away. It *would* be running away. It would justify them in believing all the things they said about him were true. He could not slink away leaving this cloud about his name. If it took his last penny, he would see this thing out. This stupid tangle of malice and lies was bound to fall apart to disclose the nothing at the heart of it. He would stay. He would endure. Yes, he would stiffen his moral muscles and endure this silly backbiting. He faintly smiled as the memory of some words came back to him from his childhood: 'Sticks and stones may break my bones, but words can never hurt me.' He tried to tell himself, he tried to believe, that it was largely his imagination. (But that was before he saw Harry.)

The problem was never finally solved. The argument went on in his mind, day after day, week after week, swaying him this way and that. But each time he decided to stay, he was strengthened by his resolve and was buoyed up with a calm assurance. Strong in his intention (before disgust and desolation again swung him the other way), he was no longer ashamed to meet Mrs. Thrale's quickly-veiled glances.

Goodness knew whether it was her own loneliness or his that Mrs. Thrale was considering, but certainly he was seeing far more of her than he had anticipated. He could not quite tell how it had come about, but every evening now, when their modest meal was cleared away, she joined him in the drawing-room, sitting demurely in the chair opposite, always with some work in her hands. She would stitch away companionably without talking, while he read his paper. But it struck oddly on his eye to glance up and see her there. It was a little stab at his heart each time, reminding him of Editha. He resented her being there, but the woman was so harmless he did not see how he was to turn away without hurting her feelings.

The first time it occurred she had found him pacing the room, pulling at his under-lip. She stood hesitantly in the doorway:

'Am I disturbing you?'

'No, that's all right,' he said. 'Just working out a problem,' he went on, indicating the chessboard with a few pieces arranged on it in the corner of the room. 'What can I do for you?'

'I wonder if it would bother you, Doctor, if I sat down here very quietly under the lamp. I've been trying to darn these socks for you, but the light is so poor downstairs that I really can't see.'

He said quickly, 'Of course, of course. But you shouldn't be —' He broke off before he finished the thought aloud. For, though it seemed rather dreadful that this woman should have to mend his socks, he could not imagine who would mend them if she didn't. Who had mended them when Editha was alive? he wondered, for he could not remember ever having seen her at this homely task; the picture of Editha did not go with ragged socks. 'It's very kind of you,' he concluded lamely.

'Not a bit of it,' she assured him, and with a little laugh added, 'I'm afraid you wouldn't take it very kindly if I mended your black socks with brown wool, and your brown ones with blue. Which was what I did last night, and had to unpick it all this afternoon.' She broke off a length of wool and began to thread a needle. 'But don't let me interrupt you, please, or I shall feel in the way. Do go on with your problem.' She raised her head and looked at him with a comprehending smile. 'My husband used to play chess.'

Yes, that was how it happened. And after that it was simple for her to slip in every evening with her meek bundle of mending. Till he got accustomed to the feel of her there, so quietly in the corner of the room, with the lamp shining down on her hair and her hands busy with a piece of stuff — a restful, motherly pose to bring comfort to a man's heart if it was sad or weary.

One evening he lowered his paper and looked across at her.

'I was thinking of asking a few people in to dinner one night next week.'

She looked up for a moment and then bent her head again over her work and took several more stitches before she answered. Then she said slowly, 'Of course, Doctor. If that is what you want. I'll manage it somehow.'

If her answer astonished him, he was careful not to show it.

'Would it be too much for you, do you think?'

She sighed.

'No, Doctor, I'll see to it. Perhaps I could get someone in to help me. I do hope you won't think I'm making difficulties, but, you see, I didn't realize when I came here that you would be entertaining quite so soon.' She hesitated long enough for a flush to come into his cheek, but she was staring down at the work on her knee. 'It was wrong of me to have told you right at the beginning, but I was afraid that if you knew ... ' Her voice died away. Then she looked straight at him and went on bravely, 'The fact is, I'm not as strong as I led you to suppose. It's my heart. I'm not supposed to — ' She smiled weakly and stopped.

'What's the trouble?'

'This silly old leaky valve,' she murmured. 'It's just the strain of bending and lifting, I'm afraid. Stupid of me,' she added with a pretty flush. 'But of course I can manage a dinner for you; I can plan so that most of it can be prepared in advance.'

'We'll see,' he said. 'We'll leave it for the time being.'

It was thus the project was indefinitely shelved. Obscurely it was a relief to him. He had been absolved from putting his friends to the test: it would have been unbearable if they refused his invitation; whatever their excuses, he would not have been convinced they were genuine.

The days passed, monotonously uneventful. Apart from his meagre list of patients he saw no one. Once, at his prep school, he had been sent to Coventry; the uncomprehending misery of those days, the unhappiness of that little boy, came back to him now in his enforced solitude. It had the effect, by degrees, of making him unreasonably nervous of meeting people he knew. He acquired the habit of raising his hat brusquely and hastening past with a sick inward flinching from the look in their eyes.

Even Miss Duncton no longer haunted his surgery. Indeed, he had not seen her since that evening in the beech copse. He tried to tell himself that it was because the girl was embarrassed by her confession, but in his heart she too had joined the army of accusers. Mass hysteria, mob emotion, he told himself drily.

But Catherine kept away because she was afraid. The cottage, which for so long had seemed a prison to her, now became a refuge into which she shrank from the impertinent questions of her neighbours. She knew what people thought. However much she protested — it did no good to protest — they continued to believe that she and the doctor had met that night by assignation. People had such beastly minds. It made her face burn with shame. What would he feel, if what they were saying should come to his ears? With all that had happened — between truth and lies — she wondered if she could ever meet his eyes again. It seemed to her that the least she could do was to keep strictly out of his way until the wicked gossip had died down; as it was bound to do in time when they saw there was nothing in it.

She threw herself feverishly into housework: scrubbing, polishing, cleaning, long after the last speck of dust had been whirled away and the oldest brass handles leaped out of the corners like a sunbeam, as if she was using this frantic energy to rub away her darkest thoughts. For, like a ju-ju victim, she was all the while pining inside. She longed for the sight of him. She wanted him to know that she stood by him. She imagined — oh, all kinds of foolishness. And all she had to treasure was the memory of that last encounter, as precious to her as a fragile bubble of glass; and as light changes the shape and colour of a glass ball, so the continual play of her imagination over that incident altered it beyond recognition to suit her changing moods of hope or despair. She even had the folly to expect some sign from him. And as time passed she drooped more and more noticeably.

'My dear, must you work so hard?' said Eve Verney on one occasion.

'I like it,' she said.

'But what is the point of all this drudgery? You're simply letting yourself go. It's dreadful, at your age.'

With a guilty smile Catherine tried to conceal her broken nails in the folds of her skirt.

'It keeps me from thinking.'

'Yes, I know, you're unhappy. Anyone can see that. But, my dear child, that's not the way to — '

'Oh, please,' said Catherine in a stifled voice, jumping up and turning away.

Even old Mr. Duncton remarked on it in his acid manner.

'I cannot imagine why you have to drag about as if you were an old woman of fifty. Are you ill?'

'No, Father.'

'It isn't very agreeable for me to have you looking so unkempt. Your hair hanging down in that uncared-for way, and that dirty old skirt. There are holes in your cardigan. Did you know?'

'I've been working, Father; cleaning out the woodshed.'

'You look as if you've been sleeping there. Is it really necessary to make yourself so doggedly unattractive? Now, don't scowl at me, I only tell you this for your own good.' He chuckled faintly. 'How do you suppose you will ever get a husband if you go around looking such a slattern?'

'The supposition doesn't arise,' she said between her teeth. 'There is no one for me to marry.' She uttered a sharp mirthless laugh. 'If there were, you'd soon find a way to prevent it.'

'Your poor father ventures to give a word of advice and gets his head snapped off,' he said plaintively. 'You're hard, Goneril. Have I ever stood in the way of your happiness?' He put on a pious, injured expression. 'Your dear mother would weep if she could hear how you speak to me. You think I'm a selfish old man. You tell yourself that I've ruined your life. But you're wrong. Show me the man who wants to marry you, and I'll not stand in your light, I promise.' And long after she had left the room, he continued to shake gently with inward mirth. He could never resist the pure enjoyment to be got out of teasing the silly girl; and, poor old man, he had so few pleasures.

★   ★   ★

Harry honourably observed the letter of his contract with Editha. But once she was dead he considered there was no longer any reason for him to keep away. Moreover, the pitiful little sum he had screwed out of her was gone. Vanished, in unlucky speculations. It had been little enough, heaven knew, to start afresh with somewhere else when, as he had pointed out to her, it was purely to oblige her that he was going. To get even that much had been like trying to bleed a heart of stone.

Well, it had all turned out for the best. He had been quite reluctant to leave the good little Toots. It was an offence to his nature to leave a piece of work unfinished. And there she'd been, the little Toots, begging to be plucked. How glad she'd be to see him again! For by this time she must have given up all hope, she would have come to believe that after all he had let her down, that he had never intended to return. He imagined with a conscious glow of virtue her delight when she saw him once more. He had not written during his absence. He didn't believe in letters. The wisest, the kindest, thing was to let it die as quickly and painlessly as possible, if he was never going to see her again. Better for her not to know where he was, that was only inviting trouble. And now, as it turned out, the silence would only make her relief at his dramatic return more intense. To settle into a comfortable marriage, with nothing to worry about, would suit him grandly — for a time.

And then there was Robert. Robert, he felt, might prove to be a great help to him. He liked Robert. His first thought was to drift round to the old stone house at once, but second thoughts are best, and he decided to wait till he was in the picture before approaching him. He considered it safer to find out what the set-up was first.

Always thoughtful of other people's feelings, he chose a day when this housekeeper person of Robert's was out. No keyholes.

He walked quietly round the house. It was not his way to go to the front door and ring the bell. One never knew what one might be inadvertently interrupting. A little mosey round first.

Robert was in his surgery. He tapped on the window and saw Robert's head jerk up, startled. Nervy, Harry diagnosed approvingly. A good sign.

Robert was surprised to see him, but more affable than he had expected. He could not know that Robert was in a state to welcome the company of a grizzly bear.

'My dear fellow,' he cried. 'Come in! What brings you to these parts?' But even as he said the words, the smile faded from his face. Harry wasn't smiling either.

He said gravely, 'I came as soon as I

heard. I've been abroad,' he added.

Robert said, 'I couldn't let you know; I had no idea where you were.'

'My dear old boy, I attach no blame to you for that,' he said generously. 'Still, it came as something of a shock. After all, we were much the same age. Poor old Ede, she was pretty rough on me sometimes, but death, I always say, cancels all debts. Hard luck that she should be the one to go and I, the rotten one, left ... I say, is there anything to drink in the house? It's a bit upsetting, isn't it?'

Watching Robert pour out the whisky, Harry observed, 'You're not looking too bright yourself. Been through a bit of a bad time, I gather. Oh, don't bother about wetting it, I'll take it as it is. Poor old Ede,' he said again, raising his glass in a sort of toast to the dead, 'she's out of her troubles! I wonder,' he went on, taking a quick swallow, 'what made her do it? No, don't tell me if you'd rather not,' he added hastily, putting up a hand. 'I shouldn't have asked,' he continued with an air of great refinement. 'I've no right to inquire into whatever private troubles lay between you.'

'What makes you conclude that your sister killed herself?' Robert said frigidly.

Harry opened his eyes very wide.

'Didn't she? Am I on the wrong tack altogether? That is why I've come, Rob, old man; to learn what really happened. I've had nothing to go on but the newspaper report of the inquest. Frankly, I couldn't understand the verdict. I know the reports of these affairs are pretty garbled as a rule, but it seemed clear enough from the evidence what had happened. Although you appear to have done your best to cover it up. It was quite a dodge to destroy the page from your Drug Book. Though I'm not sure it was entirely wise,' he added pensively.

'Oh?' Robert said in a level tone. 'Why?'

'Well, it does seem,' Harry said in a friendly manner, absently tipping some more whisky into his glass, 'as if that was the only piece of definite evidence — one way or the other. Now no one can ever know whether there were six tablets in that box, or twelve. Except yourself.'

Robert regarded him in silence.

'But I'm not disputing that you did what you thought best. Not being in possession of the facts, I'm not in a position to. But I can see that to leave the issue in doubt may have seemed the only way.'

Robert said, 'What did you really come here for, Harry?'

'But, my dear chap, simply to hear from the one person who might be supposed to know something of the matter an account of how poor Editha met her death. After all, I am her only relative.'

'You are suggesting that I knew more than I told the coroner? In fact, that I deliberately falsified the evidence, is that it?'

'Good heavens, Robert, you talk as though I was a policeman! I'm the last person to blame you. Why, the one thing old Ede was for ever dinning into me was the absolute necessity for a doctor to avoid the merest breath of scandal. Naturally, it wouldn't do you any good if it got about that your wife had committed suicide. I do understand that perfectly.'

'Nevertheless, I'm afraid you'll have to take my word for it that I did not conceal evidence or perjure myself. If I had believed Editha had killed herself, I would have said so. I don't think she did.'

Harry emptied his glass and stared into it thoughtfully.

'That seems to be the general opinion in the village too,' he remarked casually.

Robert looked up sharply.

'I thought you came straight here.'

'Well, not quite as straight as all that,' Harry murmured demurely. 'To be frank with you, it was what I heard in the village that made me decide to come and see you, Robert.'

'Ah, now we see the point of all your conjectures about suicide,' Robert said with a quietly angry smile. 'Well, it isn't necessary to pursue it. I'm perfectly aware of their conclusions on the subject.'

'Are you? I beg leave to doubt it.'

'Now what are you driving at?'

'That it doesn't do to be too naive, Robert. Simplicity can be dangerous.'

'I fail to understand your meaning.'

'You think people are cold-shouldering you because they believe you drove your wife to suicide. But they don't, Robert,' he said gently, and squirted a dash of soda water into his glass. He looked across at his brother-in-law. 'They think you killed her.'

Doctors have quiet faces. They learn early to mask their thoughts before their patients and it quickly becomes a habit they carry over into private life. If Harry expected Robert to betray himself with a start or a protest or changing colour, he was disappointed.

Robert rested the clean spatulate finger-tips of one hand on the edge of his desk. The silence prolonged itself.

'Kind of you to tell me,' he merely said at last with flat irony. 'So eventually we come to the truth.'

Harry said with an air of sincerity, 'I hope so. It isn't very pleasant for either of us, is it?'

'Where do you come into it?' Robert asked with what for him amounted to rudeness.

'As I have to keep reminding you; she was my sister.'

'Then may I remind you that you never cared tuppence for her while she was alive, except for what you could get out of her. Forgive me if I can't quite believe in this concern for her now she's dead. I don't see what you hope to make out of it.'

'Always so ready to believe the worst, you good people,' Harry chided gently. 'The fact is, I'm shortly getting married, and we're expecting to settle down here. The bride has a small property in these parts, you see. All very nice, I'm sure you'll agree. But no one wants to begin their married life in an atmosphere of undetected murder. I thought between us we could clear the matter up. All that is needed is a little more positive evidence that in fact poor Ede took her own life.' He shot a quick surreptitious glance at his brother-in-law. 'My idea was that, talking it over quietly between ourselves, you might hit on some trifling but significant detail that had heretofore slipped your memory.'

'I see,' Robert said slowly. 'I think I understand. Let me make sure. You mean, it would help if I recalled something like — the hundred pounds you had from Editha on the day she died.'

Harry stared for a long moment and then burst out laughing. Robert watched him gravely between narrowed lids.

'Now, how did you find out about that?' he chuckled. 'Lucky Jim! I collected that

242

drop of gelt just in time.' He seemed to become aware that Robert was not sharing his amusement. 'Lucky in more ways than one,' he added. 'It puts me well in the clear, doesn't it? Anyone can see that I had no reason to do for the old girl,' he added with a provoking grin.

'Can they?' said Robert. 'I wonder.'

'Poor old Ede,' said Harry on a different note, 'she was dead scared about it. I remember so well almost her last words to me: 'If Robert finds out, he'll kill me.' Yes, 'he'll kill me' was what she said,' he repeated soberly.

'The police would be interested to hear that, I fancy,' Robert said grimly, and his warm dark eyes were suddenly as cold as iron. 'You'd better get out now, before I kick you out. Nothing's too low for you, is it? You'd even use your own sister's death as an occasion for blackmail. I used to think Editha was unduly hard on you; now I see every word she said was right.'

Harry looked absurdly offended. He said in a sentimental voice, 'Oh, no, you've got it wrong. I assure you. Ede and I understood one another. The only trouble was we were too much alike. What she hated in me was really what she hated in herself. That was what she was ashamed of, not me. Poor old Ede,' he sighed, 'what a muck she made of her life!'

'Clear out!' Robert said between his teeth. 'Clear out quick!'

When he had gone, Robert flung wide the windows and let the boisterous wind rush in. Too deeply inside himself for him to recognize the source of his rage was a sick disgust with himself. He felt in some way befouled. It gave him a perverse satisfaction to realize that he had added a dangerous man to his enemies. It was as if subconsciously he welcomed the prospect of disaster.

He was too restless to settle to his work again. On a sudden impulse he slammed out of the lonely house, which was all at once abhorrent to him; and, getting into his car, drove in aimless fury away from the detestable village.

He drove half across the county before the long steady curves of the landscape began to exercise their soothing effect. Then, in reaction, he was seized by an appalling weariness; drawing into the verge, he leaned his head on his arms across the steering-wheel. He reminded himself dully that he had had nothing to eat, and after a while drove slowly on, looking for somewhere he could get a meal.

Presently he came to a whitewashed pub, bare and unattractive. He went in and ordered a double whisky. It was dark, bleak and stuffy, with varnished tables and horsehair benches. Two or three workmen leaned against the bar. They didn't serve food, the landlord's wife said, but suggested doubtfully, daintily scratching among the fuzzy clumps of her 'perm' with a pencil, that they might manage a sandwich. He mumbled that it didn't matter, thinking that a couple of whiskies would brace him enough to drive on to some more appetizing eating-place. But when he glanced at his watch after a few more drinks, he saw that it was half-past eight and too late already to be served with a meal anywhere. It didn't matter. He wasn't really hungry; the desire for food had left him.

By closing time he was astonished to discover that he was quite unsteady. 'Must drive carefully,' he warned himself as the car leapt forward recklessly into the dark.

He got back all right. But he omitted to turn on the light as he entered the house. 'Dark as hell in here,' he muttered, and lurched into the console table. Down it went, the great bowl of Michaelmas daisies crashing on top of the telephone, the salver ringing as it span in flattening circles to the ground. Dr. Mansbridge staggered, tripped, and went over the lot like a tree.

Mrs. Thrale woke from her first sleep with a start of terror, though in truth the noise was less like burglars muffing an entry than elephants paying a social call. She pulled on a wrap and ran to the head of the stairs, calling in a trembling voice, 'Who's there ... ? What is it ... ? What's happened ... ? Is that you, Doctor ... ?' When no answer came, she nerved herself to switch on the lights and go down.

The doctor was lying among the fragments of china and water from the broken bowl with his head pillowed on the bottom stair. His eyes were shut. For a heart-stopping moment she thought he was dead. When she tried to raise him he groaned and moved his head so that an abominable odour of spirits came to her nostrils. She drew back in disgust. He was drunk, the filthy pig! Well, she wasn't going to put him to bed, he could just lie there. She drew her skirts about her and swept upstairs, outraged. But under her prim feminine horror a minute germ of power corrupted in her mind, spreading like yeast secretly and astonishingly as the days went by.

The events of that night were never mentioned between them. Presumably, he thought, she knew nothing about it. He invented a poor little story to account for the overturned table and she pretended to believe it. At all events, the incident had the curious effect of making her even more attentive to his welfare than before. She was wonderfully considerate, wonderfully thoughtful in the little things she did for him.

One night a couple of weeks later, he was roused by a tapping on his bedroom door. He grunted, 'What is it?'

The door softly opened and Mrs. Thrale murmured, 'It is I, Doctor.' He heard the rustle of silk as she approached, and switched on the lamp. Mrs. Thrale stood by his bed in a pretty silk dressing-gown with her hair spread over her shoulders and some soft white stuff showing at the opening of her wrap.

'Forgive me, doctor, for disturbing you,' she began in a husky, breathless voice.

'What is it, Mrs. Thrale?' he said brusquely, sitting up, his hair tousled boyishly with sleep.

She gazed at him, large-eyed.

'It's my heart,' she said in a soft, panting voice. 'I'm feeling so ill ... I had to come, I was frightened.' Her wrap fell apart as she caught his hand and pressed it to her breast in its thin covering. 'Just feel my heart, doctor,' she exclaimed in that strange husky voice, and fell against him.

He snatched his hand away from that warm, soft, throbbing flesh.

'Mrs. Thrale!' he said sharply. 'You shouldn't have come here! Go back to your own room, and I'll come and examine you there.'

'Don't send me away,' she murmured. 'Don't you want me to stay?' She clung to him, her soft hair brushing his cheek. 'Don't you like me at all?' she whispered.

He was appalled. He pushed her roughly away.

'Oh, don't be so cruel,' she breathed. 'Couldn't you care for me a little?'

'This is outrageous! If you don't know how to behave yourself, you'll have to go,' he said, his face burning.

'You drunken beast!' she exclaimed, with a suddenly venomous look. 'No wonder your wife killed herself!'

He said harshly, 'Leave my room at once! I'll speak to you tomorrow.'

The recollection of that ugly scene was to turn him hot with embarrassment for many a day. A man feels uncommonly foolish in the role of Joseph. There is nothing heroic about repulsing a woman. Sexual virtue in a woman may be admirable; in a man, it is faintly ludicrous. He might have felt even more wretched about the affair if he had remembered that old tag about hell knowing no fury like a woman scorned. But he never paused to wonder what excuse she would make to her friends for being turned out bag and baggage at a moment's notice.

She turned it to her own account all

right. She arrived back at the vicarage, wrought up, white-faced, on the point of collapse. As soon as she was alone with her friend she burst into tears.

'Forgive me, Nell, forgive me! I had to come to you, I had nowhere else to go.'

'My dear,' said Mrs. Wellcome, patting her gently. 'What is the matter?'

'It's so frightful ... I don't know how to tell you ... I was so terrified. I just ran out of the house ... I thought he was drunk at first. He drinks, you know,' she interposed, raising wet blue eyes to her friend. 'One night — oh, most disgusting! — he came home so much the worse for drink — no, really, one can hardly bring oneself to speak of such things! — that he knocked over the furniture and passed out in the hall. I found him lying on the floor.'

'Dr. Mansbridge?' Mrs. Wellcome said incredulously. 'I can hardly believe it! He never used to drink. I suppose it's grief for his wife.'

'Grief!' exclaimed her friend with a cynical smile.

'My dear, what *did* you do?'

'I left him there, of course. If a man

behaves like a beast,' Mrs. Thrale said spitefully, 'why shouldn't he sleep on the ground like one?'

'What a horrible experience for you, my poor dear,' Nell Wellcome agreed quickly to assuage a faint qualm of guilt. 'You do believe that if I'd had the least idea I would never have suggested your going there?'

Mrs. Thrale pressed her hand tenderly.

'How could you know? I don't blame you, dearest. I didn't think it mattered much anyway. After all, when a woman is alone in the world and has her living to earn, she can't be too critical of her situation,' she said with wry self-pity. 'I decided to be sensible about it. I thought I could manage. Till last night.' Tears thickened her voice again, and she struggled to compose herself. 'When he forced his way into my room, I thought he was drunk, you see.' She shuddered and pressed her handkerchief against her mouth. She closed her eyes and said in a stifled voice, 'The man must be a sexual maniac ... '

'Delia! You don't mean ... ?' cried Mrs. Wellcome aghast.

Mrs. Thrale nodded, gazing at her friend

over the handkerchief.

'It was frightful,' she whispered. 'Like fighting with a wild beast.' She burst into sobs again. 'I *couldn't* stay there, Nell, I couldn't. I locked my door, but you can imagine I didn't go to bed again; and as soon as I dared I crept out of the house.'

'My dear! My dear!' murmured Mrs. Wellcome, putting her arms about the weeping figure. What a dreadful thing to have happened to poor Delia. Of course she must stay with them — but, Mrs. Wellcome admitted to herself with a sinking heart, Herbert was not going to be pleased, and really she did not know how she could tell him what had occurred, it was frightful. Really frightful.

9

The Occasional Shivering
Note of an Owl ...

In the High Street, outside the ironmonger's, stood Miss Barnaby and Catherine Duncton with their shopping baskets. They were both red in the face.

Catherine, that meek girl, so tentative towards her elders, had just flashed out, 'I don't believe a word of it!'

Miss Barnaby said:

'Well, really! You're not suggesting I made it up, I hope. I tell you I heard it from her own lips.'

Catherine said with insensate rudeness: 'Then she was lying.'

'Well, really!' Miss Barnaby said again. 'Considering ... ' She broke off and laughed. (Miss Lucas was going to love this!) 'Excuse me. I'd forgotten he was a special friend of yours. Of course you wouldn't want to hear anything against him.'

This was malice. This was deliberate cruelty. Catherine's voice trembled with indignation as she retorted:

'No, I don't. I don't want to hear any more lies about him. Hasn't there been enough harm done, slandering him behind his back, poor man? Even criminals are given the chance to defend themselves. I don't know how people can be so wicked!'

Miss Barnaby smiled pityingly and leaned forward to pat the girl's arm.

'He's lucky to have one such loyal friend.'

'It's just that it's so terribly unfair,' Catherine stammered. 'That dreadful woman, why is she allowed to go round saying these monstrous things? Someone ought to stop her!' she declared wildly. 'Surely, Miss Barnaby, you don't really believe it? You must know it can't be true.' Her voice shook.

Miss Barnaby said glibly:

'Of course no one wants to believe such dreadful things about another person. But, you see, it would be equally horrible to believe that poor Mrs. Thrale wasn't telling the truth, wouldn't it? If you knew her ... She's such a nice creature. It's impossible to think she should have invented such a preposterous accusation. Why should she, after all? Why, she'd be rendering herself liable to prosecution.'

'I'll never believe it. Never,' Catherine declared.

'My dear,' Miss Barnaby said gently, 'you're very young. I'm afraid you don't know what men are like.'

'Perhaps not. I do know what women are like, however,' she said brusquely and walked away, her heart thumping with rage.

It is easy enough to rush to the defence of someone on the spur of the moment: it is not so easy to shut the slander from one's mind afterwards. And Catherine could not forget it. She refused to believe it; but she could not prevent herself from trying to imagine what had happened. She imagined — oh, horrible things! Useless to wrench her thoughts away, they returned of themselves. She wanted to run to Robert and beg him to tell her the truth. That, of course, was impossible. She visualized with extreme clarity a little scene, sharply denned as in a camera obscura, in which she was standing by the desk in his surgery, declaring with passion her confidence in him. He was extraordinarily touched. He took her hands in his. 'My dear,' he said. 'Oh, my dear. You're very young. I'm afraid you don't know what men are like.'

* * *

People were beginning to experience a faint boredom with the Mansbridge affair, till Mrs. Thrale's little story brought it throbbingly to life again.

As Mrs. Ambrose remarked:

'Each new revelation about Robert astounds me more. It makes me feel I never knew him at all. Really too extraordinary! That quiet little man.'

Cum grano salis,' said her husband. 'The woman was obviously hysterical.'

'Can you wonder?'

'You mistake my meaning, dear. I doubt if her report is really trustworthy.'

'Do you mean to tell me you don't believe it?' Mrs. Ambrose said indignantly. 'Then why did she have to leave so suddenly?'

He shrugged. 'Perhaps he gave her the

sack.'

'Really, James, you're impossible! Why on earth should he? A nice woman like that.'

'We haven't heard his version of the story,' he reminded her.

'Oh, you men! How you all hang together! It's revolting!' Mrs. Ambrose poured herself some more coffee and sipped it thoughtfully, watching her husband crackle his newspaper. A gleeful idea presented itself to her. 'James, listen! Why shouldn't we ask Robert to our cocktail party on the eighteenth?'

'Steady on!' remarked Mr. Ambrose.

'It would be a perfectly proper thing to do. After all, he is a friend of ours, and one ought to stand by one's friends. It would show we had faith in him. And think what fun it would be to see all the old tabbies sitting up.'

'Rather risky, don't you think? It might be a bit uncomfortable. Why not ask him to a quiet little dinner to begin with, or something of that sort?'

'Oh, no. That would be horribly awkward. One wouldn't know what to say to him. But a cocktail party's different. There's

257

no opportunity for serious talk. It would break the ice for him. And only think how fascinating to watch everyone's reactions. Do agree!'

'My dear, you will do what you want, whatever I say. You only want me to concur so that you can blame me afterwards if things go wrong.'

'Beast!' said Mrs. Ambrose amiably, and hurried away then and there to scribble a little casual friendly note to Robert. Telephoning would have been clumsy.

It never entered her mind that Robert might decline the invitation. She was deeply chagrined by his refusal. Mortally offended. Till she decided that it was a plain indication of his guilt that he could not face all his old friends, and then she felt better.

$$\star \quad \star \quad \star$$

For Robert, the invitation had come too late. Now he was suspicious of all gestures of friendship. He no longer believed in their sincerity. Even a few weeks earlier he might still have been able to brace himself for the ordeal, but their eyes had avoided his face for too long. It left him bitter. It was as though his skin had been flayed raw and was too sensitive to bear a touch. This unintroverted man would never have believed he could feel such painful disillusion. He no longer had any desire to see the people he had once regarded as his friends. The thought of them filled him with loathing and contempt.

The incredible part was that the weight of their silent accusations actually afflicted him with a queer uneasy sensation of guilt that he could not shake off. It was the odd irrational feeling of the outcast that the herd must be right in its judgment, because the herd was the majority. In some way that he did not know, but they knew, he was to blame. Well, damn them all! Let them leave him alone: that was all he asked. He only wanted to be left alone. With the instinct of a wild animal hiding itself from man.

It was this ever-growing acceptance of his guilt (and surely, he argued with himself, if he had been the right sort of man, with the power to believe in himself, he would have been able to combat the lot of them and establish his innocence beyond conjecture?)

which sapped his courage.

As the days grew briefer with the turn of the year, he acquired a habit of taking long solitary walks, meandering desolately by the river a mile or so beyond the town. There was nothing to break the monotony of the level grey fields but a few wind-twisted willows or a single brick dwelling in the distance. Its bleakness was its attraction for Dr. Mansbridge. One rarely ran across a soul down there. Sometimes a farm labourer riding home to his tea on his bicycle. Or a group of schoolchildren chattering shrilly and lurching clumsily together as they walked. Or a dirty coal barge, disturbing in its passage the slow-moving pattern of transparent black shadows on the oily greenish-brown water flecked with sky-white.

Dusk would fade the last colour from the scene. The willows would turn black, like tea-leaves splashed against the sky. At last the birds too would fall mute. Soon there would be no sound but his own steps and the occasional shivering note of an owl. Only the red spot of his cigarette glowing among the deeper shadows. This was the moment he craved for, as a person in intolerable pain craves for a drug: night hid him from himself and he could at last discard the mask of consciousness he had worn all day. He became an anonymous man strolling in the dark, breathing in the night-scented air, thinking of nothing.

It could not always be as simple as that though. He discovered other ways of escaping from the consciousness of his own identity that pressed in on him so painfully, binding him to a nagging awareness of the failure of his personal life. In alcohol there was always a moment when he found release from present, past, and future. It was even worth the bad taste it left in his mind the next day, the unpleasant taste of a bad conscience. He thought at times with horror: 'I'm becoming a drunkard. I'm letting them drive me to drink.' Then, ashamed, for days he would keep off the bottle.

But virtue must have a purpose, and Dr. Mansbridge had lost his self-respect before he began to drink. You might say that it was because he had lost his self-respect that he drank.

It was the old woman who came to clean

up for him who gave him the idea of apply-
ing to a registry office for someone to look
after the house properly. ('Folks living like
pigs … Emp'y bockles everywhere … Ain't
'e got no sense?' she grumbled.) Doubtless
from some private superstition of her own,
the queer old body never addressed her
employer directly, indulging instead in a
perpetual muttering monologue of admoni-
tion and complaint, whether he was there to
hear her or not. Such orders as he gave, she
took in gloomy silence — and disregarded.
Usually he paid no attention to her, scarcely
comprehending her mumbling jargon; but
this time, by dint of repetition, he grasped
what she was grumbling about, and was
so shocked by the old biddy's disapproval
that he actually went off and considered
the suggestion.

He had not meant to take on another
housekeeper; the abominable Mrs. Thrale
had thoroughly sickened him of the
prospect. But a registry office, that was
a different matter. He wondered that he
had not thought of it for himself. They,
of course, would be able to find him a
proper servant; he would stipulate for the

old-fashioned kind who knew her place and stayed in it.

They sent him Ada Bantry, an Irish girl about thirty. A coarse-looking wench, but cheerful and willing, with an easy Irish habit of agreeing with everything he said.

True, she was not very great on the cooking. Boiled potatoes and a chop, or a piece of bacon and cabbage, were the extent of her powers. And if she swept the dirt under the carpet, well, where was the harm in that? Sure, she was satisfied if he was. It was not at all a bad place, for all her apprehensions. The good St. Joseph had listened to the prayers of a poor lonely girl and sent her somewhere she could find a bit of comfort. Wasn't it the great blessing to have come to a house where the master liked his drop to drink? There was always something left in the bottle for herself.

Of her own accord, Ada used to put an open bottle at his elbow when she brought up his luncheon. At first, he let on to be displeased in his cold English way, making out he didn't drink with his meals.

'Ah, sure, it's a comfort to a man when he's tired out with listening to people's troubles and pains,' she said easily. 'And where would be the harm in it?'

'A great deal, if I go to my patients smelling of drink,' he said crossly.

'And who could think the worse of you for that? Haven't a doctor the same rights as another man?' she demanded with a great show of indignation, so that he was obliged to smile.

Sometimes he would be feeling too weary and depressed to resist taking a drink or two. The girl was right. It was a comfort. Nice, good-hearted, sensible creature.

But it was amazing how quickly a bottle emptied itself once it was broached. Maybe Ada was a little careless. Once he noticed her remove a bottle that still had a couple of liquid inches curling round its glass hump. He called her back and pointed it out to her.

'It have so,' she agreed, holding it to the light. 'Would ye be wanting me to save ye this drain?'

'Well, don't throw it away.'

'I'd not do that, sir. Trust Ada Bantry,' she said lightly.

He looked at her sharply, a reprimand

in his mouth, when he was assailed by a sudden realization of his own hypocrisy. How mean to grudge the girl a little drink, when he indulged himself as much as he wished because he had the money to pay for it. He held his tongue.

It never entered his mind that Ada was encouraging him to drink. He only felt relieved that she should understand and take it as a natural thing that a person should feel the need of a drink. Disapproval made for an uncomfortable atmosphere, particularly the sour unspoken disapproval of a servant. He was actually a little pleased to know that she drank too. It makes for an odd kind of friendliness to share the same taste with someone, even with someone totally inappropriate. It made him feel not so desperately lonely and desolate. She might be sluttish in her work and unattractive in her person, but she had a natural sympathy for the weaknesses of human nature that made one like her in despite.

One evening he was feeling so bored that when she came in with a fresh siphon he said impulsively, 'Don't go, Ada!'

She turned.

'Sir?'

'I want to talk to you.' But he could think of nothing to say. What on earth did one talk to such a girl about? 'Have a drink,' he said. Her broad face with its red varnished cheeks split into a smile that showed her ugly yellow teeth.

'I'm obliged to you, sir.'

'Well, sit down for a minute. Tell me about yourself.'

''Tis lonely for you, sir, night after night,' she said naively, 'with never a soul to speak with. I have the homesickness too.'

'Tell me about your home,' he said.

★   ★   ★

Sometimes on his solitary riverside walks he ran into Catherine Duncton, as innocently as if it was by chance she was there. It was dreadfully hard to find something to talk to him about naturally after so long, but she went at it with desperate perseverance. And in some way these vapid conversations were not unpleasing to him. It eased his spirit to find there was someone, even if only a silly moonstruck girl, who still treated him with respect.

She no longer cared what people thought; her only wish was to save him. It shocked her to see how he was deteriorating physically. If she could bring him back his self-respect, she asked nothing else. He must be vindicated. There was something in his eyes that reminded her painfully of a trapped fox she had once seen, wounded, helpless, dying, yet masking its misery with a terrifying savagery. An unbearable commentary on life.

To see him so wretched roused in her a more intense love, a passion of longing to repay him for all he had suffered, a yearning so keen as to be a physical pain at her heart. It was hard to talk of unimportant topics and see his indifferent weary eyes. But she had learnt a great deal in these last months.

*   *   *

All that winter he passed his evenings with the servant, Ada Bantry, drinking. It was better, more amusing, than drinking alone. Ada was companionable; and, after a few drinks, became rowdily merry. Her laughter rang into the street. She liked to dance to the radio. The neighbours were scandalized. Passers-by could see her bouncing about through the lighted windows and the doctor roaring out tunelessly and banging his glass on the arm of his chair. You would have thought it hardly possible for the neighbours to be more scandalized. Drinking with his servant! And worse, no doubt.

He developed a brusque and irritable manner with his patients, as though he resented their troubling him. Sometimes he bluntly refused to go out at night when he was called.

Gradually, even those patients who were still loyal to him from past gratitude began to turn against him. Once the wife of one of his patients rang his bell a little before midnight. He threw up his bedroom window and leaned out.

'What is it?' he called.

The woman stepped back and looked up at him. Her dim moonlit face was frantic, distraught; tears glittered on her cheeks.

'It's me, Doctor; Mrs. Ferguson.'

'What is it, Mrs. Ferguson?'

'He's gone, Doctor! My Sidney's gone!' the hoarse cry floated up to him.

Well, he had warned her that the man was unlikely to live through another night. He uttered a conventional expression of sympathy and advised her to go to bed and try and get some sleep.

She looked at him in dismay.

'Aren't you going to come and see him? I can't go back there alone.'

'It's no use my coming. There's nothing I can do if he's dead. I'll come round in the morning and give you the certificate,' he said brutally and slammed the window shut.

It was quite a few minutes before her retreating footsteps echoed in the silent street. A melancholy sound.

And then a baby died in one of the cottages, because he was drunk and diagnosed as colic what turned out to be an acute appendicitis. It's the sort of thing that can happen to any doctor some time or other — doctors are not infallible — but this had happened because Dr. Mansbridge was drunk: that was different.

People turned against him in earnest then. The mad woman took to sidling past his gate at night and throwing stones through his windows. A private act of public vengeance. And the strange part was that he didn't seem to care. He sincerely tried to understand why he no longer minded the disapprobation which surrounded him. Punishment for a real wrong done, they say, no longer affects a child who has been punished too often and unjustly. Or was it merely that alcohol hardens the sensibilities as well as the liver?

* * *

In the early spring old Mr. Duncton died.

Catherine showed neither elation (which would have been shocking but understandable) nor grief (which would have been irritating but natural in the perversity of the human heart); she went about merely looking a little blanker than usual, and what her feelings were she confided to no one.

Of course she had been through a great strain for years; an unwholesome life for a girl. One could not expect her to bounce up like a ball. ('That dreadful old man ... without wishing to speak ill of the dead ... ' they said among themselves.)

Mrs. Verney always knew exactly what

people ought to do and could never resist telling them. People flopped about like stranded fishes, waiting for something outside themselves, some great benevolent incalculable Chance, to pop them back into the water. And Mrs. Verney said to Catherine plainly that she ought now to take a long holiday.

Catherine smiled faintly:

'Where would I go?'

'Anywhere. My dear child, the whole world is open to you now. You can go anywhere you choose.'

'There isn't anywhere I want to go,' she said with that small fixed smile.

'It is precisely when one feels like that, too apathetic to budge, that one most urgently needs to get away. If you don't get out of these four dreary walls you'll break down, mark my words,' Mrs. Verney admonished.

'I'm quite happy where I am, you know. And I don't think I should find it much fun in some strange place on my own. I've never been good at making friends.'

Mrs. Verney cried, 'But it's up to you to *make* it fun! You've got to learn to live your own life now.' She said vehemently, 'If I had my way, you'd go right away from this place and never come back.'

Catherine went quite pale.

'Why?'

'Well, good heavens, what sort of life can you ever hope to have here? There's nothing here for a young woman. You'll become a dowdy little spinster, who's seen nothing, done nothing, been nowhere. Get out of it, now you've got the chance. Go somewhere you can meet a few men at least, and perhaps find someone to share the future with. Don't look so absurdly shocked. Everybody ought to get married, it's unnatural not to. Do you want to sit here and let your life unwind day after day like a ball of wool, and then find when the ball is unwound to the end — *nothing*?' Mrs. Verney concluded dramatically, throwing out her hands.

Catherine looked down at her lap and made no answer. There was nothing she dared say. To utter her thoughts aloud would have been to betray them. She had an atavistic dread of speaking aloud her secret hopes for the Fates to overhear. From a childish notion that Mrs. Verney might read her thoughts if she did not turn them quickly out of her mind, she used the first excuse which came to hand.

'In any case, it's no good thinking about it: I can't afford to take a holiday just now.'

Mrs. Verney said with deep concern:

'Do you mean to tell me that your father's death has left you badly off?' And seeing Catherine squirm, added, 'You mustn't think I'm merely being inquisitive; but if you'd rather not tell me about it. I shall understand.'

'It's not that. There really isn't anything to tell. It's my own fault for being so stupid. I hadn't realized Father was living on capital. He never spoke about it. I suppose I ought to have known that all old people have to live on their capital nowadays: I just never thought about it; I'm such a fool.'

'You're not telling me he's left you penniless?'

'We don't know yet exactly how much is left. There's something called Probate. There'll be the cottage, of course.'

'Oh, was it your father's? I thought it was only rented.'

'Yes, it is, but the rent's very low and the

solicitor says they can't turn me out.'

'But, my poor child, what are you going to do?'

'Oh, I shall be all right.'

'Of course you will,' said Mrs. Verney with determined cheerfulness. 'We'll find you a job, don't worry. Have you thought at all about what you could do?'

Catherine said vaguely, 'Oh, there may be quite a bit for me to go on with, the solicitor says.'

'Yes, but Catherine, you must be sensible. You can't just sit here with your hands folded until all the money is spent. You ought to use the money to get yourself trained for some career. Everybody's trained today. It's hopeless otherwise.'

'I don't think I'm clever enough to be trained for anything,' the girl said with a quite maddening humility, as though such simplicity was something to be proud of. There is really nothing so exasperating as those who won't be helped. Mrs. Verney flung up her hands.

'My good child!'

Catherine said quickly:

'You mustn't bother about me, Mrs.

Verney. Something will turn up, you'll see. I'm not worrying.'

Catherine was not such a dunce as she pretended; to simulate a mulish stupidity was often the easiest way out of an awkwardness. And Catherine had no intention of letting herself be pushed into some job. She did not want people busying themselves in her affairs. She did not want them even to have their eyes on her; she wished to remain as unnoticeable as she had always been. What she was going to do would be quite tricky enough without being unnerved by the consciousness of being spied upon and gossiped about: it would be like trying to walk a tightrope with birds flying around to distract one.

In her imagination, the scene was to take place on the river-bank as dusk fell, and the most difficult part would occur in darkness so that they would hardly be visible to each other. But though she went there day after day, Dr. Mansbridge never appeared. A steady dejection seized her. Twice she walked past his house at night and heard a woman's high raucous laughter above an incredible clatter of cans being kicked around and dropped and cats wailing, which she knew to be the late-night dance music on the radio. And the sound, the sound of that woman's laughter, was like having a knife stuck in her guts; she imagined that a knife in the guts would be a tearing pain composed of first an icy shock and then a burning, spreading out fiery fingers ...

She was not unaware of the stories going round about him, and they filled her with anxiety, for himself as much as for her. It would be too frightful if he fell into the hands of that atrocious woman. She made up her mind that she would have to go to his house to see him. There was simply nothing else for it.

She went at night — when the streets were empty and there was no one to observe the rare passer-by. He opened the door to her himself. Coming from a lighted room, he could not discern who it was standing there in the dark.

He said:

'Yes? What is it?'

He seemed surprised when she told him who she was, and it only then struck her that it was a strange hour to pay a call.

'What's the matter?' he said sharply.

'Oh, nothing. That is, I mean there's nothing wrong with me. I just wondered if I might speak to you for a few minutes. I'm ... But perhaps you're busy ... '

'It's late,' he said.

'Yes. I didn't think ... Perhaps you'd rather I came some other day,' she said, suddenly longing to escape while there was still time. But he opened the door wider and said:

'No. Come in.'

She stumbled through the dark hall, making automatically for the lighted room. She stood there blinking at the sudden brightness, seeing the newspaper on the floor where he had dropped it, the glasses on the table, the gross-looking, red-faced servant staring at her.

Catherine turned quickly, with an expression of furious distaste on her face as if she had been spat on, and said to the doctor:

'May I speak to you alone?' in a tone that made it a command.

He said, without looking at her:

'Cut along, Ada.'

Ada pushed her feet into her shoes and

stood up. 'Will I get the lady something to take?' she offered hospitably. 'A cup of tea, now?'

Catherine ignored her stonily. She did not move until she heard the door shut. Then she faced him and smiled.

'I'm afraid I've disturbed you,' she said, to see how he would excuse himself. But he offered no explanation, he merely said indifferently:

'It's of no consequence. What did you want to see me about?'

'I want your help ... your advice ... ' she murmured, stroking the tabletop. 'There's no one else I can turn to now ... now that Father's dead.' She raised her head and looked full at him with her large luminous eyes.

'Won't you sit down?' he said.

She gave a little laugh.

'I'm nervous,' she confessed. 'It's difficult.' She clasped her hands. 'But I must try not to be stupid about it.' She took a deep breath. 'You see, when Father died there was very little money left. I hadn't realized ... It means that I shall have to get a job of some sort. Only, you see — ' She spread out her hands with a helpless look. '— I'm not trained for anything. Mother died while I was still at school, and I left to keep house for Father; and ever since, as you know … ' She stole a glance at him: he was regarding his locked hands between his open knees. 'There doesn't seem to be anything I can do, except look after people.' She waited for him to speak, and after a moment he roused himself to say:

'There are plenty of people who want looking after.'

'Yes, I think there are,' she agreed softly. 'I thought perhaps I could get a post as a housekeeper.'

Again there was a pause. Catherine watched him pour himself a drink.

He swallowed a mouthful and then asked, 'And how do you want me to help you?'

'I thought — I thought — ' She stammered. ' — perhaps you might … ' She paused and tried again. 'You might know of someone, or something,' she concluded lamely.

He gave a brusque laugh.

'My dear young lady, I'm a doctor, not a registry office.'

'I'm afraid I'm being very tiresome,' she said quickly, and fumbled with the buttons of her coat. 'It was only that I so dread the idea of going to a complete stranger. I thought if I could be with someone I knew … someone like yourself,' she added shyly, 'it wouldn't be so bad.' She ran her tongue across her lips and made a pitiful little sound like a laugh. 'I suppose you wouldn't consider taking me on, yourself?'

He said roughly:

'I already have a housekeeper.'

Catherine said:

'You could get rid of her.'

'Get rid of her!' He stared. 'Why on earth should I?'

'Only that — I suppose it sounds awful cheek — but I'm sure I could make you much more comfortable than she can.' She ventured a small, nervous laugh. 'I dare say you don't notice the way the place is kept, but really — ' She turned her fingers over to show the dust on them from the tabletop. 'It's not the way a doctor's house should look, is it?' She clasped her hands together. 'Please forgive me for what I'm going to say, but you really ought not to let her sit in here with you, drinking.'

'Why not?' he inquired drily, pouring himself another whisky.

'You don't know what dreadful things people say.' She shuddered and put her face in her hands.

'They can hardly say much worse than that I killed my wife.'

At this laconic observation she looked frightened. Above the hand clasping her mouth, her eyes stared, pale and immense. She muttered something faintly through her fingers. And then suddenly she wrung her hands together and burst into tears.

'Oh, damn this girl!' he thought and drained his glass. He said, 'I'm sorry if I frightened you.'

In her sobs he heard her say, 'I didn't know you knew ... It's so wicked ... so cruel ... I can't bear it ... I can't bear it ... '

He said sardonically, 'You seem to think I'm not a murderer.'

She gasped: '*Oh, don't!*' She went to him, tears raining down her white face. 'Listen to me ... you must listen,' she implored, shaking his arm. 'You mustn't give way ... You're so *fine*! Don't let them beat you down with their wicked lies … Please! Please … Can't you understand that when they see you behaving like this — letting yourself go to pieces, drinking, hiding away from everybody — it makes them think that all the hateful things they've invented about you must be true after all … ' He looked down at her without expression. 'You don't believe me,' she said hopelessly.

'I believe you,' he said. 'But, you see, you've got the wrong end of the stick: I'm supremely indifferent to their opinion.'

'That's not true,' Catherine said in a low voice. 'You do care. And that is why you drink. Isn't it?'

He glowered at her.

'Isn't it?' she insisted boldly.

With a total effect of unexpectedness, his sombre face broke into laughter.

'I'm very gratified by your interest, Miss Duncton, but now I think you should go. It's late.'

'You're angry with me.'

'Not at all. But it's late for a respectable young lady to be visiting a disreputable widower.'

'Don't speak of yourself like that,' she

cried. 'You don't mean it. You say it because it hurts you.'

'What a romantic young woman you are,' he said drily. He went towards the door, carrying his glass with him, and said in a dismissive tone, 'I'm sorry I was not able to be more helpful.'

She still stood in the centre of the room, the unkind light throwing ugly shadows down her face.

She said very softly, 'I wish you'd let me be helpful to you.'

'Kind of you. Now you must run along.'

She said, 'I don't want to go,' in so low a voice that he hardly caught the words.

He said with weary patience, 'My dear young lady, you can hardly stay here.'

She was not looking at him, her head was bent and she was lacing her fingers tightly together.

'I can't go — ' she made a gauche but not unexpressive small movement with her locked hands — 'like this with nothing settled.'

'Settled? Settled?' he repeated. 'What is there to settle?'

'I didn't mean that exactly. I put it badly.

I mean — I want — If you would let me help you to — to — ' She glanced about her wildly. ' — to get back to — as you were. '

He said sardonically, 'To get back my self-respect, you mean. And how do you propose to accomplish that impossible feat?'

She said on a note of humble desperation, 'Oh, why must you always speak so unkindly! It makes it so difficult. I don't know how to say it when you look at me like that.'

'I'm sorry.' He turned away and occupied himself in filling his glass again.

She said breathlessly, the words tumbling out, unselected, audacious:

'I thought — of course, I know you don't care for me ... I'm not thinking of that ... just ... I thought it would show people ... they would see ... If we could be married, I mean ... ' Her voice shut off abruptly once the tormenting words were out.

For a long while she listened with a blank mind to her heart racing the ticking clock.

He squirted soda into his glass, and then held it up and eyed her with an ironic smile over the rim.

'It's a charming idea; but, frankly, I prefer

to remain as I am: sodden with drink and self-pity.' He emptied the glass and set it down. 'I've always thought that Don Juan was probably a very weak character, more sinned against than sinning. A man only needs to have a bad reputation, for the women to come swarming round to reform him. I don't know why it should seem so attractive to redeem a hopeless person.'

Catherine said in a trembling voice, 'You think I'm not serious.'

He said roughly, 'I think you're a bloody romantic little fool!'

'I'm not. I swear I'm not. I know what I'm doing.'

'Oh, go home!'

'No, I won't go. I won't leave you.'

'Look here, my dear girl, get this into your head: I don't love you and I've no intention of marrying you, or anyone.'

'What are you going to do with your life, then?'

'I shall go quietly on in my sour disgruntled way, thank you very much.'

'No! You shan't give in. I won't let you,' she said desperately.

'Must we go on with this? Must we?' he

repeated wearily. The clock struck. He said, with a horrified face: 'Look at the time! For God's sake, go home!'

'I don't mind being compromised.'

'God, but you're stubborn! I think you must be a little bit mad. Can't you understand that I don't want my life to be any different? I don't care what happens any more. I'm angry, embittered, and finished. And you light-heartedly propose to picnic in the ruins.'

Catherine said with deep intensity:

'You don't want your life any more: give it to me.'

10

A Fabrication of Hideous Nightmare

Mrs. Fitzalan glanced up from her detective story and abstractedly watched her husband making his nightly preparations for bed. She smiled to herself. Custom could not prevent her finding an elderly man taking such pains with his appearance a little ludicrous, a little pathetic. And they say women are vain, she thought to herself, watching him fiercely massage bay rum into his scalp. Yet she knew it was not from sexual vanity that he expended so much effort, but in the same spirit as an Empire-builder dressing for dinner in his lonely outpost: a matter of stern self-respect.

She glanced down at the printed page again and, after a moment, murmured from some association of ideas:

'I've never seen a man alter so much as Robert since his marriage.'

'How d'you mean?' grunted the colonel

absently. And added: 'He's certainly pulled himself together.'

'I suppose he has in a way.' Mrs. Fitzalan put her finger on the page to mark her place. 'That wasn't really what I meant. He's so *different*. He never used to be sarcastic. He was always such a friendly chap; now he's got a trick of speaking almost like poor Editha.' Mrs. Fitzalan sat upright in bed and stared at her husband with glittering eyes. 'That's exactly how he speaks. How extraordinary!'

The colonel didn't answer, being occupied in swinging his arms about and counting under his breath with the absorbed attention of one performing an intricate religious ritual.

Mrs. Fitzalan returned to her book, not to read but to meditate, with her eyes on the page. Of course everyone had been very curious about the marriage, and of course with the passing of time old scandals died down, but Catherine had really been very artful in the way she got Robert socially accepted once more. She began so modestly with little tea-parties at home when Robert was out (and after all, everyone agreed, there was no earthly reason why *she* should be cut off from all her friends); and then there were a few dinner parties, and of course he had to be invited too, that was understandable. But no one now could feel the same towards him. Besides, he had changed — oh, utterly!

She looked up to say:

'Henry, did you notice how her eyes kept turning to him all the time? I rather wonder if he's pulled himself together as much as you think. She was watching to see how much he drank, I believe.'

'Damned silly thing to do. Puts a fellow's back up when his wife interferes over a thing like that. Especially in public. Makes him feel a fool.'

'Did she? Did she actually say something, Henry? I never would have thought she'd have the nerve. She looks half scared to death of him.'

'I was just taking the shaker round. I said to Robert, 'Let me top that up for you, old man,' something of that sort, and the stoopid girl put a hand on his arm and said, 'Don't have any more, Robert dear.' Made the chap feel a perfect fool.'

'What did he do?'

'I passed it off. I said, 'Oh, nonsense, there's not enough here to drown a fly,' or something like that, and filled up his glass. Robert said, 'If you're afraid of my getting drunk, why insist on bringing me to these affairs?' And the girl went white.'

'You see, she is afraid of him. Oh, poor little thing!'

'Why the dooce did he marry her?' said the Colonel.

Mrs. Fitzalan sighed.

'Why did *she* marry *him,* is more ponderable, I suppose she had some romantic notion, poor child. But, really, she can't have understood what she was taking on. No wonder she looks so scared.'

'She's no right,' said the colonel unreasonably, 'to go around letting people see that she's frightened of him. What's she afraid of, damn it? He's not going to kill her!'

'What a perfectly dreadful thing to suggest, Henry,' his wife said indignantly.

The colonel paused in amazement with his teeth half out of his mouth. He really was *damned* if he understood the way women's minds worked.

★   ★   ★

Janet sent Betsy Golding's baby an antique silver rattle that Miss Ryder had let her have at cost price. She seldom saw the Goldings since she had left the school, and she scarcely ever thought about Ned. The episode — it had only been an episode — had become part of the bittersweet past; and she was absorbed in the present. Crispin was teaching her to sculpt; in return, she helped in the shop, which in its way was fascinating too. She liked Crispin enormously: it was funny she was not more popular generally when she was such an interesting and clever person. Miss Ryder, too, was frightfully kind to her. It was like having a home again after many years, without the usual drawbacks of home life.

Curiously enough, Naomi was not in the least jealous of Janet. She understood, and was gratified by, Janet's admiration of Crispin. It was proper that Crispin should have someone to appreciate her at her true worth. And it was agreeable for them both to be able to talk 'shop' for hours together. She was such an intelligent girl, and so helpful in the business. It was like having a daughter in the house. It might be sentimental and absurd, but she and Crispin really did regard Janet as their daughter. They actually felt a glowing pride if Janet looked prettier than usual. Sometimes, Naomi wondered if it was not a little dull for Janet. She ought to meet people of her own age, go out more; it could not be much fun for her, always cooped up with women of twice her years.

'We ought to try and find a few young men for Jan, don't you think?' Naomi suggested to Crispin.

'Where does one find such animals in this neck of the woods?'

'We should be able to rustle up one or two. What about General Ridley's nephew?'

'He's abroad, unfortunately.'

'Or young Topping.'

'My dear!' protested Crispin, laughing.

'The Dixon boy, then.'

'He's just got engaged. Didn't you see it in the paper last week?'

'Well, how about Mrs. Verney's son? Not

very sparkling, but better than nothing — to begin with. We might ask him and his mother in to supper one night.'

'Young Jan'll liven him up if anyone can,' Crispin said with a smile.

★   ★   ★

Mrs. Petrie often felt dazed with the rapidity of her experiences. She scarcely knew whether she was happy. Often she was very unhappy and humiliated; but in a strange way she enjoyed her sufferings, for life had become so real and vivid. 'Yes, this is Life,' she felt in the most painful moments and it gave her an extraordinary sensation of exhilaration, as though she had been granted the precious possession of some secret knowledge. Harry continually outraged her ideas of decency, she was often terrified of what she might discover next, yet his bland amorality fascinated her. And she could never be certain that in one of his cold rages he would not walk out on her for good. She learnt to placate him at any cost; there could be no feminine tantrums for her. She did not dare to contemplate what her life would be without him now. He had her in thrall, all right. She was in passionate subjection to him. She looked back on her past life with incredulity; a year ago it had been as flat as a lake, now it was like fighting tremendous seas which broke over her thunderously, knocking her half-senseless, dragging her down against the grinding shingle; one struggled out of it breathless but intensely alive. It was frightening and wonderfully exciting.

★ ★ ★

When the great desire of her heart came true, Catherine believed she had nothing else to wish for. She was frighteningly happy. For their honeymoon, she chose to go to Cornwall, to a small village not ten miles from Falmouth, where there was nothing to do all day but fish. Robert was to be happy, too: the rest of her life would be spent to that end. She lay in the grass, her arms behind her head, watching his grave profile against the slowly stirring leaves, content to lie there feasting her eyes on him. She was as patient and quiet as a cat at a mousehole, so still that for long stretches at a time he became unaware of her dreamy doting gaze. He could sit for hours together suspended in a tranced alertness without conscious thought. Then she would re-cross her ankles, or push aside the feathered grasses with her hand, and the slight movement would be enough to recall him to himself, and he would turn his head and murmur half-guiltily with a crooked smile:

'All right?'

'Perfectly,' she would answer, stretching out her hand for him to touch.

Useless for Robert to venture a quick kind pat; she would grip his fingers ardently in hers, stroking his palm with her thumb. He was sufficiently sensitive to her feelings to know she was hurt when he gently withdrew his hand. It was better to pretend he had not seen the gesture, better to say quickly:

'Sure you're not bored?'

Then she would shake her head and smile.

'No, darling. I'm quite happy. I love to sit here and watch you.' Presently, she might add: 'It doesn't bother you, my being here, does it?'

'Of course not.'

'Sure?'

'Quite sure.'

'Then please kiss me.'

When he leaned to embrace her, she clung to him as desperately as if it were a farewell kiss, and then with an effort would break away and say tremulously, 'Now you must get on with your fishing and forget about me.'

If only once he had answered, 'I can't forget about you.' But he never did. Walking back to the hotel arm in arm, she would ask him what he thought about all the time.

'Nothing,' he always answered.

That she could not believe. She longed for him to turn on her a teasing glance from those warm eloquent eyes of his that would say as plainly as words: 'What do you think?'

But he never did.

She yearned to hear him say just once that he loved her.

But he never did.

It was unreasonable of her to expect it.

She knew before she married him that he didn't love her. Had she some fond foolish hope that once they were married he would learn to love her? Perhaps the miracle of her achievement made her confident that with patience and tenderness she could achieve anything she really desired. Hadn't she learned that nothing was impossible?

She was timid with her caresses, having already discovered he did not like to be touched. But it was hard to keep her hands off him. She so desperately needed reassurance. She could not restrain herself from asking whenever he fell silent what he was thinking of. At any time a foolish question. As foolish and irritating as the other pitiful plea that she could not prevent herself uttering — 'Happy?'

It should have been satisfaction enough for her that he had stopped drinking altogether. For a time — perhaps the length of the honeymoon — it did gratify her immensely. Just as long as she continued to believe that it was due to her. But presently doubt crept in. It had been too sudden, too easy; she apprehended that he could as easily have stopped any time he wanted to, only the desire to do so had been lacking. He hadn't needed her. What she had pretended was the justification of their marriage was proved nonexistent. She found it in herself to wish that there had been a long, arduous struggle to cure him of alcoholism, for then his dependence on her would have been a power in her hand. As it was, her one poor little weapon was blunted, useless. He did not need her. The knowledge made her nervous. She became acutely sensitive to his every word and gesture, as though she expected him at any moment to accuse her of marrying him under false pretences. Which was absurd.

For Robert was really behaving very well. He was as nice as could be to her. Only, he didn't love her. He wanted her to enjoy herself (it was, after all, her honeymoon; he had had his twenty years ago, and there could be no other for him). Despite her insistence, he refused to spend all the time fishing. There was little enough to do in such a small place, but he did what he could to make it pleasant. He took her on excursions to places of interest. They went to the cinema and saw ancient blaring films.

They went for long walks. He was just as nice as could be. Only, he didn't love her.

He did his best. She was his wife. She was young, and pretty, in a way that unfortunately didn't happen to attract him (his taste was for skin-and-bone women with fiery eyes and a sleek elegance about them in all their attitudes: but Catherine was a nicely rounded girl; Catherine was without temperament, one could almost say, lymphatic; there was no mystery there, no fire, to quicken the pulses), she was gentle and appealing and he could not but be touched by her transparent adoration. Until he began to be irritated by it.

Few things are more terrible than to find oneself pursued by the relentless hunger of someone begging for crumbs of love that one has not got it in one to give.

The less he had to give, the more frantically she abased herself. A honeymoon is one thing, but he could not pretend to something he did not feel for ever. She was always being wounded and going out of the room to hide her tears. 'What did she expect? For God's sake, what did she expect?' he asked himself petulantly, between boredom and guilt. Could she not grasp that a reasonable man of middle age was as little inclined to lovemaking across the breakfast table as he would be to stand up and strip himself naked in a public place or shout obscenities at the top of his voice in church? The one was as unseemly, as unthinkable and embarrassing, as the other.

Catherine had believed that she had reached the end of all her desire in her marriage; having Robert, there could be nothing else she could want. She had yet to learn how painful it can be to live in closest intimacy with someone you love who doesn't love you. It was like fairy gold, which a human will buy with the highest price he can pay, only to find when he opens his hand that he has got nothing. Catherine was tortured with longing for his affections. She did all she knew to win him. She would have done better not to try so hard. True, she counselled herself to be patient, not to let him see that she was hurt by his indifference. But each wound, she found, went deeper, and was less susceptible to healing.

The wound he had given her when they returned to the old stone house was still suppurating. Ever since Editha's death, he had slept in the spare room he used as a dressing-room when they were married. He continued to sleep there now. He said he had got used to it. He said he liked sleeping alone. He said there was less likelihood of her being disturbed if he was called out at night. Yes, that hurt. But there was something worse than that, something she could not mention to him. If, at least, he had let her have his room, it would not have been so bad; but he insisted on her having the main bedroom; that, he said, was right and proper. And she could not tell him that she hated it. She could not tell him she was afraid, that she did not want to sleep in Editha's room, in the bed on which Editha had died.

She did murmur palely that she didn't quite like the idea of sleeping in a bed where someone had died. And he said with a trace of impatience that Editha had not died of anything infectious. Of course, he was not imaginative. She would never have dared to confess that for her the room was haunted by Editha's presence. Her scent seemed to cling about the room, in the curtains. But even after the hangings had been changed, the scent still hung around and would drift to her from an open drawer. Or so she fancied.

No, Robert was not imaginative, he was not sensitive. What do widowers feel when they get into their first wife's bed to make love to their second wife? Evidently, nothing. To Catherine, it was like making love in the presence of a third person, so that she sweated with the horror of it. The only way to avoid that experience was to go to his room. And that had its own awkwardness, that too could make her sweat, for she dreaded a rebuff, or even that he should think she was importuning him. All this did nothing to ease her tension, her starving need of him: a need that was emotional rather than sexual; but it is hard for a young woman in love to distinguish between the two or to find a satisfaction for the one except through the other. How else could she gauge his feelings for her but by his embraces? Even his embraces could not satisfy her hungry heart, but at least they stopped for a little its wretched persistent whining, like a beggar's babe. It was to stifle its cries that she sought his embraces.

His heart sank at her amorous wiles. He came near to loathing her when she fawned on him. Yet even when she saw his face stiffen with a minute muscular contraction she had learned to read, she could not stop herself: the need to overcome it drove her on despairingly. She could not let him alone. The more she pursued him, the more he withdrew into himself. He took to shutting himself into his surgery of an evening on the pretext of work. Once she made an excuse to go in there and found him playing chess, with a bottle of whisky beside him.

'Oh, Robert! Darling! You haven't started drinking again!' she exclaimed with great reproachful eyes.

'I'm not 'taking to drink', I'm simply having a drink.'

'Of course, darling. I know you wouldn't take too much. I only meant, is it wise to start again?'

He closed his eyes wearily.

'Don't run me so damned hard,

Catherine. Let up just once in a way, won't you?'

'Darling, I have to look after you. That's what I'm here for.'

'Is it?' he said and leaned his head on his hands.

'What's the matter, Robert?' she gently asked.

'Why must anything be the matter? Why must there always be something the matter if I want to be alone or I want to have a drink?'

'You told me you were going to work, that's all. When I saw you weren't working, I wondered if something was wrong, perhaps. That's all,' she repeated.

He caught her by the wrist and swung round in his swivel chair till he was facing her.

'The first essential for all good wives to learn, my dear, is tact.' He smiled up at her unkindly.

'How have I — ' she began.

'And the second is to know when to drop a subject,' he said, letting go of her wrist. And as she was leaving the room, he called after her, 'Don't sit up for me. I may be late.

I have a problem to work out.'

She paused and looked back at him. He was pouring some more whisky into his glass.

'What sort of a problem, Robert?'

He came back from a long way away.

'Well, now, what do you suppose?' he said with an effect of elaborate patience.

She tried to think what he could mean. What sort of problem that she could know about? Her eyes wandered round the room.

'A chess problem, do you mean?' she said uncertainly.

'Yes, that's it. A chess problem, dear,' he said, drawing the board towards him.

She suffered from the unacknowledged belief that her marriage was a failure: the fact was that she did not understand how to manage a husband. She came to feel that he hated her. And she was afraid.

Robert did not mean to be unkind. He reproached himself for snubbing her, but the satirical words had snapped out before he could prevent himself. She irritated him in the same way he had irritated Editha. People noticed it. They noticed how her eyes uneasily followed him about the room, turning away hastily when he glanced in her direction. They saw the weak, timid smiles she gave him, like a child hoping to placate the incomprehensible sternness of an adult. It was so evident to everyone that she was afraid of him, that some people wondered whether she had uncovered some deep and dreadful secret about him that would account for her look of misery. The thought excited in them a rich rewarding glow of compassion. They watched eagerly to see what was going to happen. Possibly, vultures follow the doomed from a sense of pity; possibly it is in the nature of some pious rite that they gravely swoop down to pick the flesh from the bones of the dead, and not a simple act of carnivorous lust.

One evening in late autumn, Robert was seated at the centre table in the drawing-room, sucking his pipe and musing over a letter he was writing. Catherine was sitting on the floor by the hearth, leaning against the old green armchair with a book open in her lap. But the page was in shadow. She sat in a cave of darkness illuminated by moments with the flicker of flames from the fire. She felt relaxed and peaceful.

Catherine put out a hand and touched the table, as if to assure herself by its solidity that the moment was real. The movement caught Robert's eye. She was so quiet he had almost forgotten she was there. He glanced towards her with an abstracted smile. The smile encouraged her. She could hardly expect a better opportunity.

She said, 'Robert!'

'Mmm?' He pressed his finger into the bowl of his pipe.

'I'm going to have a baby.'

The pen dropped from his hand and rolled across the paper, leaving a track of small blots down the sheet.

'What?'

She could not make out his expression. She said nervously, 'I'm afraid I'm going to have a baby. Do you mind?'

'Do I mind?' He laughed. 'Kate, darling!' The table rocked as he sprang to his feet and came towards her. 'It's the most wonderful news I've ever heard!' He took her hands. 'Is it true? Are you sure?'

She nodded, too tremulous to speak. It was the first time he had called her Kate.

'I was afraid you wouldn't want it.'

'Not want my boy? Bless your heart, there's nothing in the world I want more. This calls for a celebration. We must drink to him.' He was laughing, but his eyes were wet. He jumped up and flung open the doors of the cellarette. 'It ought to be champagne,' he said taking out the various bottles and scrutinizing them. 'Nothing less than champagne is good enough to welcome young Mansbridge into the world. We must never let him know that his first health was drunk in mere Amontillado, he'd never forgive us.' He fetched two glasses and began pouring in the sherry, talking excitedly all the while. 'What shall we call him? I should like to call him Michael, after my father. What do you say, dear?'

'Suppose he isn't a boy,' she murmured, smiling in response to his effervescent spirits.

He said indignantly, 'I shall suppose no such thing. Are you trying to undermine his self-confidence? Of course he'll be a boy. What else could he be?'

She couldn't help laughing at his absurdity.

'A girl.'

He was astounded.

'A girl! But that's an absolutely staggering suggestion. Such an idea had never occurred to me. That would necessitate a radical reconstruction of all my plans.'

'What plans, darling?'

'It would be useless for me to put her name down for Winchester, for instance. I wouldn't want a daughter of mine to turn out a hearty soldierly type. A *daughter of mine* ... Yes, that has rather a charming sound, too. Shall we drink to Michael and Kate, then?'

'Michael *or* Kate,' she amended, laughing.

'To both of them!'

He handed her the glass and as she looked up to take it he saw that her cheeks were glistening like glass in the firelight.

'My dear,' he said and dropped on his knees beside her. 'My dear, what is it?'

'I can't help it. I've never seen you happy before. I thought I never should.'

He gathered her into his arms.

'Oh, my poor girl!'

'I thought you wouldn't want the baby because it was mine.'

He was wrung with pity.

'How could you have imagined such a thing?'

'I thought you hated me. I thought you were never going to forgive me.'

'Forgive you? What had I to forgive, my dear? I should think it is for you to forgive me.' He tightened his arms round her. Her cheek was against his. She said:

'I only did it for you, my darling; I wasn't thinking of myself.'

'I know, dear.'

She leaned sideways to use the handkerchief in his breast pocket to dry her tears.

'I couldn't believe you were happy, but I didn't know for certain that you weren't until that time you said to me, 'If only I were free!''

He looked down at her with a puzzled frown.

'I said that?'

'Of course you did. Don't you remember? It was the day you told me you were going away. I was so miserable, darling; because it meant not seeing you any more, no more rides into Cambury. You can't imagine what they meant to me. I knew it made no difference to you — probably it was only a bore to you, though you were always so sweet to me — but I was desolate. And then you said that about being free.' She gave him a nervous smile.

His brows were drawn together.

'But what — ?'

'It was because I loved you so much, dearest, that I wanted you to have what you wanted.' She pressed her eyes into his shoulder. 'And then it all went wrong.' He could feel her body shaking against him.

He said gently, stroking her hair.

'There, there, my girl! Don't think about it anymore. It's over and done with, and from now on everything's going to be all right.'

The tears came out in a flood.

'You're so good to me! And, oh, God, I've been so wretched! When I discovered what everyone was saying, I was absolutely terrified. Not for myself, darling, but for you. I didn't know what to do. To see what it was doing to you ... Oh, God! To watch you going to pieces ... I thought my heart would break ... '

He could scarcely catch the sense of the words sobbed out in little gasps and muffled in his coat. He could not tell whether it was her heart or his that was beating so loudly between them. He said, with a faint frown of bewilderment:

'But what are you blaming yourself for, my dear? You weren't at the bottom of that slander.'

She sobbed out:

'How could I know they'd think it was anything to do with you? I meant it to look like an accident.'

He was surprised to find he was sweating. He pulled her arms away.

'Let me go, dear; you're strangling me.'

He got to his feet and stood with his back to her, fumbling along the chimney-piece for his pipe. Catherine was lying with her face in the seat of the green velvet chair, her body twisted into a Z. In that twisted body was the beginnings of a child; his child; the child he had always wanted.

After a moment, he was able to say quite steadily:

'What was to look like an accident?'

She raised a flushed wet face, started to speak, and then stopped. She turned pale. In a voice hardly above a whisper, she said,

'Why do you look like that?'

'What had you to do with Editha's death?' he said in a parched voice. He became aware of a pain in his hand. He was gripping the chimney-piece so hard that the edge was cutting into his fingers. 'Answer me!'

'N-nothing,' she stammered, fixing enormous strained eyes on him.

'You said you meant it to look like an accident, but it all went wrong. What were you talking about?'

She shook her head dumbly. She looked both surprised and frightened, as if she found herself without warning sinking into a bog.

He heard himself utter the incredible words in a voice that was toneless with horror:

'You killed her ... You murdered my wife ... Didn't you?'

Still with that numb stare, she muttered:

'I thought you knew.'

He gave an abominable laugh.

'You thought I knew!'

'I thought that was why you hated me,' she whispered, plucking at her lips. She dropped her forehead into the heel of her palm and groaned in a sort of prayer: 'What have I done? Oh, God, what have I done?'

Still it seemed to him impossible. He could not believe in murder. He could not believe that this quiet timid girl had cold-bloodedly, deliberately, done to death a woman she scarcely knew, who could never have done her the least harm. It must be a joke, a joke in very bad taste. To believe otherwise would be to accept that life was without purpose or reason, a fabrication of hideous nightmare.

He said sharply:

'She died of an overdose of sodium amylobarbitone. Where did you get it from?'

She put her hands over her face.

'Dr. Horace had prescribed it for Father. I emptied the powder out of the capsules and filled them up again with crushed aspirin for Father. I put the powder in the peppermint creams.'

Relief broke out in him in a sudden sweat. It occurred to him that the whole thing was a fantasy of her overwrought mind, due to her condition.

'Sure it was in the peppermint creams?' he said.

She nodded anxiously.

There was nothing in the peppermint creams, my dear. They were analysed and found to be innocuous.'

'I put it all into one,' she said quickly, 'so that if — I mean — she might not have eaten it, but if she did … '

'If she did, it would be sure to kill her.'

'I didn't — It wasn't —' she stammered. But how could she explain that it hadn't seemed like that to her? To poison only one sweet in a bagful was not like murder at all; it was just a sort of lottery — a deadly lottery.

Robert said heavily:

'You couldn't have known she was going to that fete. You couldn't have known she would buy those peppermint creams from you, even if she did come. How did you induce her to take them?'

'I didn't. You did. Don't you remember, you promised me that you would come and buy some sweets from my stall. You told me you never ate sweets yourself.'

'I bought fudge,' he said hoarsely. 'I remember quite well, I bought fudge.'

'You asked for fudge, but you never

unsealed the bag to see what I'd given you. Even if you had, you'd only have thought I'd made a mistake, wouldn't you? Even if you'd brought them back … '

A groan burst from him.

She was upright on her knees before him, clinging to the edges of his coat, and crying frantically:

'You mustn't hate me, Robert! It was for you I did it. Only for you. I didn't care about myself, I didn't care what happened to me. I only wanted to set you free, because I knew what it was like to be in a trap. I wasn't thinking of myself, I swear to you! I couldn't know, could I, that you would marry me in the end?'

He was married to her. He had married the woman who had killed his wife. And by some terrible jest of Fate she was to bear his child. It had the unbearable horror of some old Greek play.

To Catherine it was like breaking her hands against a stone image, a stone image with a face that was a scream of anguish.

She sobbed, 'I tried to tell you, Robert. In the wood that night. I wanted to tell you then. I thought that was why God had brought us together there. But you wouldn't *listen*.'

He knocked her away. The name of God on her lips was the last blasphemy.

She fell. Tears and blood mingled on her cheek. She crawled to him and clutched his legs.

'Robert!' she gasped.

He said in a terrifying voice:

'Let go of me! Get out of my sight!'

Her face, smeared with blood, swollen with tears, was hideous with terror.

She cried out:

'Robert ... Don't look at me like that ... What are you going to do ... ? Robert!'

★   ★   ★

It was very cold, crouching there on the floor, with the wind blowing in and the front door banging to and fro with the sound of a hammer dully knocking nails into wood ...

We do hope that you have enjoyed reading this large print book.

Did you know that all of our titles are available for purchase?

We publish a wide range of high quality large print books including:
Romances, Mysteries, Classics
General Fiction
Non Fiction and Westerns

Special interest titles available in large print are:
The Little Oxford Dictionary
Music Book, Song Book
Hymn Book, Service Book

Also available from us courtesy of Oxford University Press:
Young Readers' Dictionary
(large print edition)
Young Readers' Thesaurus
(large print edition)

For further information or a free brochure, please contact us at:
Ulverscroft Large Print Books Ltd.,
The Green, Bradgate Road, Anstey,
Leicester, LE7 7FU, England.
Tel: (00 44) **0116 236 4325**
Fax: (00 44) **0116 234 0205**

Captain Guy Conway of the British Secret Intelligence sets out to investigate Fortune Cay, a three-hundred-year-old cottage on the Yorkshire coast. The current owner is being terrorised by his new neighbour, who Guy fears could be his arch-nemesis, an international mercenary and war criminal whom he thought he had killed towards the end of the Second World War. En route to the cottage, Conway rescues an unconscious woman from her crashed car — only to find that their lives are inextricably linked as they fight to cheat death . . .

JESSICA'S DEATH

Tony Gleeson

Detectives Jilly Garvey and Dan Lee are no strangers to violent death. Nevertheless, the brutal killing of an affluent woman, whose body is found in a decaying urban neighborhood miles from her home, impacts them deeply. Their investigative abilities are stretched to the limit as clues don't add up and none of the possible suspects seem quite right. As they dig deeper into the background of the victim, a portrait emerges of a profoundly troubled woman. Will they find the answers they need to bring a vicious killer to justice?

WHITE WIG

Gerald Verner

A passenger is found shot dead in his seat on a London bus when it reaches its terminus. Apart from the driver and conductor, there have only been two other passengers on the bus, a white-haired man and a masculine-looking woman, who both alighted separately at earlier stops. To the investigating police, the conductor is the obvious suspect, and he is held and charged. The man's fiancée hires private detective Paul Rivington to prove his innocence — and it turns out to be his most extraordinary and dangerous case to date . . .

THE GHOST SQUAD

Gerald Verner

Mingling with the denizens of the underworld, taking their lives in their hands, and unknown even to their comrades at Scotland Yard, are the members of the Ghost Squad — an extra-legal organization answerable to one man only. The first Ghost operative detailed to discover the identity of the mastermind behind the buying and selling of official secrets is himself unmasked — and killed before he can report his findings to the squad. Detective-Inspector John Slade is his successor — but can he survive as he follows a tangled trail of treachery and murder?